SIDEWALK SPOTS

A MYSTERY NOVEL

KATHY DORSEY

FREILING

PUBLISHING

Published by Freiling Publishing, a division of Freiling Agency, LLC.

70 Main Street, Suite 23-MEC
Warrenton, VA 20186

www.FreilingPublishing.com

ISBN 978-1-950948-23-9

Printed in the United States of America

Dedication

To my husband, Terrence W. Dorsey

"I'll have no husband, if you be not he."

William Shakespeare
As You Like It
Act V, Scene IV

Any city that doesn't have a Tenderloin isn't a city at all.

Herb Caen, *San Francisco Chronicle*

There's no place like Gnome.

Marcus Plato Hanlon

Table of Contents

Foreword
Spot Check

Have you ever wondered about sidewalk spots? I have. What were they before? Who made them? Did they look down? Did they even notice if they left anything behind? Did they step on them? Or, did others step on them? What type of shoes did they wear, if any? What determines sidewalk spot size? Some people collect old coins, stamps, or works of art. I collect sidewalk spots. Collectors have to find somewhere to store theirs. I don't. I can leave my collection just where it lies.

Take a look at any sidewalk on any street, in any town or city across this country, and you'll find sidewalk spots. My friends, the ones who travel, tell me you can find sidewalk spots in Hawaii and Alaska and in all cities throughout the world. They're everywhere—from Tokyo to Toronto.

Sidewalk spots appear to be random. They are different from sidewalk stains. Spots are three dimensional. Stains are flat. I have no idea what makes up a spot. They seem to rise like phoenixes from the concrete. Yet, unlike phoenixes, none fly away. To many, sidewalk spots are blemishes. Not to me. They are my best friends.

I have never seen a spot higher than about one-sixteenth of an inch. Even though they seem to appear indiscriminately, they also look deliberate. To me, sidewalk spots look like dabs of tar. However, I've never seen anyone spoon out drops of tar on sidewalks. I am also tempted to believe that sidewalk spots are bits of residue from bilges of alien spaceships, although I have no evidence to support this belief. So I continue to wonder how sidewalk spots are made. I've asked the sidewalk spots, but they are like mimes. Even though they don't use words, they reveal themselves to me in other ways.

I have traveled to other towns and a few cities in this country. In every one, I have found sidewalk spots. All spots look like those in my town. Some sidewalks have more spots than others. Where I live, the sidewalks with the most spots are those with the most foot traffic. Yet I have never seen a foot leave a spot. To date, I have found no sidewalks without spots. They may exist, but I haven't been able to find them. And I have looked.

I have observed people who have tried to remove sidewalk spots. Unlike me, I assume they must consider them unattractive. Just for the heck of it, I tried to remove a sidewalk spot in front of my place of business and bring it inside. I couldn't get it off. It wouldn't budge. The more I tried, the more indelible it became. Rather than fight it, I decided to embrace it. Why not? A sidewalk spot doesn't require any special care or maintenance.

I believe sidewalk spots are like tattoos. Those who try to get rid of their tattoos know how difficult they are to remove. Sidewalk spots are no different. Just like a tattoo, each sidewalk spot tells a story. But a sidewalk spot story is less obvious than any tattoo story. A sidewalk spot is far more difficult to decipher. Unlike tattoos, sidewalk spots don't display colorful designs of roses or dolphins, characters such as "Mother," or traits such as "Born to be Wild." Sidewalk spots are more like Rorschach's inkblot images. If you stare at a sidewalk spot long enough, it can reveal a lot about its sidewalk and about its town or city. Just like an inkblot, a sidewalk spot can also help you get in touch with yourself.

Of course, the spots on my sidewalk do not actually belong to me, although they are now part of my collection. They came part and parcel with a business property I purchased when I moved from San Francisco to my current city. I own and operate a liquor store. Over time, I have developed a proprietary interest in both my liquor store and my sidewalk spots. I share my sidewalk spots with a bank, a restaurant, a beauty parlor, a law office, and a convenience store on my block. We also share customers, but not all of them. Some patronize the bank and the law office but not the convenience store. Some customers patronize the bank, the restaurant, the beauty parlor, and the convenience store, but not my place of business. Some customers patronize my place of business and not the others. There are no hard feelings. It's just that we offer different things to different people who have different needs at different times. Yet we all share the same sidewalk, on the same block, for the same people, at the same time.

No one else on my block seems to share my enthusiasm for our sidewalk spots. Nor do they seem to imagine anything about what these sidewalk spots have to tell. Over time, I learned to keep my interest in sidewalk spots to myself. People don't understand my fascination. Many think I'm unusual. Some think I'm eccentric. Others believe I'm obsessive. So I always tried to keep my sidewalk stories to myself until one Wednesday morning. That day, I returned to work and found a whole different set of sidewalk spots.

I noticed these new spots when I got out of my car. They were the same size as the others. They were about one inch in diameter and about one-sixteenth of an inch high. Like my sidewalk spots, they were dark. But these new spots seemed to shimmer and shake in the sunlight. They were more like gelatin than tar, and they seemed to be part of a long trail. I followed the trail from my parking place to the restaurant alley. What could they be? Could they be cherry or barbeque sauce from the restaurant?

I continued to follow the spots as far as the bank. I bent over. I touched one of the new spots. The spot moved and startled me. Then it broke and left a stain on my finger. I flinched. The stain looked more like blood than cherry or barbeque sauce. I decided to investigate further. Where did these spots come from? What did they mean? Who or what made them?

I approached the bank manager, Harvey Wilcox. He stood outside the bank. He had a coffee in one hand and a cigarette in the other. I asked him what he thought about this new trail of sidewalk spots. He just shrugged his shoulders. I knew he wouldn't let his coffee get cold or let his cigarette burn out. As usual, Wilcox didn't have time to bother with me or the spots. So I continued to follow the trail of spots past the beauty shop until I reached the convenience store. The owner, George Johnson, was standing outside. I asked him what he thought about the trail of new sidewalk spots. Like the bank manager, he shrugged his shoulders. George had never bothered with the sidewalk spots in front of his store, either. As I showed him the stain on my finger, George shocked me and asked if I had cut my finger on the broken glass in front of my liquor store.

That Wednesday morning, I found more than a trail of new sidewalk spots. I also discovered more blood, lots of broken glass, and what looked like a burglary. These discoveries changed my life forever. What or who had interfered with my sidewalks? It was a mystery that began many years ago, in another city, with different sidewalk spots.

Chapter 1
Spotlight

I live in a city called Gnome. People who don't who live here would call it a town, but for some reason, our founders opted to call Gnome a city. I don't know why. Apparently, cities are larger than towns, towns are larger than villages, and villages are larger than wide spots in the road. Nowhere could I find what delineates one from the other. My guess is elected officials make those decisions. And I suspect it sounds better to be a city than a town.

In my opinion, Gnome is nothing more than a village. Anyone from a real city, such as San Francisco, would call it a wide spot on the road to nowhere. I know because I grew up in the city of San Francisco, which, just to confuse everyone, is also the same as the county of San Francisco. Gnome is nothing like San Francisco.

For the record, Gnome has a population of about three thousand people. Russian writers such as Nikolai Gogol or Leo Tolstoy would have called them "souls." The Bible would have called them the "salt of the earth." San Franciscans would call them "hicks." I call them neighbors. San Francisco boasts a population of about one million people. Actually, it's about nine hundred thousand. Regardless, it has lots of sidewalks with lots of spots. My city has fewer sidewalks and spots than San Francisco, but it has more than the next town. Size matters when it comes to sidewalks and spots.

I moved to Gnome at the age of fifty-three. My San Francisco employer offered me an early retirement. Redundancy would be a better term. Nonetheless, I took it. After more than thirty years of sitting behind a desk doing the same job for the same company,

I knew I was ready for a change. I just didn't know what kind of change.

Anyone who has ever lived in San Francisco knows it's an expensive place to live. The cost of housing tends to get less and less expensive the farther you move away from the San Francisco Bay area. I knew if I could move at least 100 miles away, I could reduce my cost of living and enjoy an easy drive back and forth from my home to San Francisco. Because I wasn't ready to sit and do nothing, I also wanted to own a business that didn't demand too much of me.

The prospect of moving away from a city where I had spent my entire life scared me. I sought the help of two acquaintances who specialized in real estate. After a few months, one found a house and a business in the city of Gnome. It's where I find myself today.

I was unprepared for life in a small city. My first struggle was how to pronounce the city's name correctly. I assumed the name rhymed with "Nome" as in Nome, Alaska; or "Rome" as in Rome, Italy. I also assumed the city had been named after the elf-like figures that often appear in gardens. Both assumptions were incorrect.

When I first said the city name out loud, my next-door neighbor, Wally, said, "Wrong!" He was exasperated. "You must say all the letters!"

"You mean gee-nome?" I asked. I assumed there might be a correlation between the city name and genetics. This assumption was incorrect, too.

"Wrong!" said my next-door neighbor again with greater exasperation. "You must say all the letters."

"You mean gee-no-me?"

Wally smiled and said, "Now you've got it!"

I was through making assumptions. Just the same, I wanted to know how the city got its name.

Wally explained that some people believed the city was named after the small elf-like figures that people put in their gardens. I smiled. He went on to say other people believed the city was named after the genome project. I smiled. Then he said that most people believed the city was named after an abbreviated expression used by the first city inhabitants who settled here almost 170 years ago. Those people are believed to have said that once you "get to know me," you'll stay. I laughed out loud. Somehow, his explanation made perfect sense. Now I tell anyone who asks, once they "get to know me," they'll want to move to my city, too.

This is how I found myself in Gnome, where I discovered the mystery of the blood, the shattered glass, and the burglary that started in another city at another time.

If a man has been his mother's
undisputed darling, he retains
throughout life the triumphant
feeling, the confidence in success,
which not seldom brings actual success
with it.
Sigmund Freud, 1917

If only.
Marcus Plato Hanlon

Chapter 2
Spotty

My name is Marcus Plato Hanlon. I was born in San Francisco more than fifty years ago to Rita Marie Hanlon. She was unmarried, and she remained unmarried for the rest of her life.

When my mother became pregnant, her parents threw her out. Her parents deserted her when she needed them most. They couldn't stand the stain or the shame they believed she put on their name. I never met her parents, so I was unable to form my own opinion about them, nor did I get to know more about the sanctity of the Hanlon name. To this day, I wonder what was so good about their family name that caused so much grief. As much as San Francisco has always been known for its liberal beliefs, those beliefs were not shared by my grandparents. Unlike her parents, my mother never deserted me.

So it was no surprise that my mother never had much to say about my grandparents. Their outward shame became her inward shame. Over the years, I managed to glean some information from her about my grandparents. She told me they were born in the Midwest and left the corn fields of Iowa to find work in a big city. That big city was San Francisco. My mother never revealed to me why they decided on San Francisco rather than bigger cities such as Los Angeles, Chicago, or New York. Nonetheless, they settled in an area of San Francisco called North Beach. There, my grandmother gave birth to my mother. Two years later, she gave birth to my aunt, Edna Louise Hanlon.

On my own, I learned Hanlon is an Irish name. I also learned that many Hanlons originated in Northern Ireland. Most likely, the Hanlons from whom I descended immigrated to the United States during the potato famine. This is just a guess on my part. Because I do not know the given or first names of my grandparents, it's impossible to research. That's okay. I am fairly confident that, despite my grandparents' protectiveness over their family name, it's unlikely I descended from any Irish royalty. And, because my mother raised me Roman Catholic, I assume my grandparents were Roman Catholic, too. However, it's an equally good possibility their family may have come from Protestant Northern Ireland. It's just as possible my mother became Roman Catholic as a way of thumbing her nose at her parents, as if bearing an illegitimate child wasn't already bad enough in their eyes.

According to my mother, my grandfather worked for the utility company. He read meters. She didn't say if he read water, gas, or electric meters. For all I know, he could have read meter maids. It doesn't matter now. My grandmother also worked. She waited tables in a series of neighborhood restaurants and lunch counters. I am not sure if any are still in business. It doesn't matter now, either. What does matter is my mother couldn't afford to live in North Beach after I was born. We lived in an area of San Francisco called the Tenderloin. She could barely afford to live there. It wasn't until many years later, when I found a good job, I could afford to live in North Beach and return to my family "roots."

When I tell people I grew up in the Tenderloin, their eyes usually grow wide. Few people will admit they were raised in the Tenderloin. It's an area of San Francisco known to house what some would describe as the city's underclass. My Aunt Edna always referred to the Tenderloin as lower Nob Hill. It was her way of giving us and the Tenderloin some class. Geographically, she was right. The Tenderloin is just below Nob Hill. But it's lower in status. In fact, you couldn't get much lower in San Francisco.

In reality, my mother and I did not live among Nobs or snobs. Instead, I grew up around more colorful people. Some of those colorful people were black and many other shades of humanity. Many were also homosexual. They all had one thing in common: they spent every hour of every day just trying to get by, and they did it on very limited opportunities. Few doors opened to residents of the Tenderloin. Yet the Tenderloin was a part of the city where they could afford to live, at least most of the time. It wasn't a neighborhood demarcated by white picket fences. It wasn't a neighborhood where you could find parks, schools, or children at play when I was a boy. Instead, the Tenderloin was a neighborhood of single room occupancy apartments. An apartment like ours was rare. We had an extra room with one bed in which she and I took turns when it was time to sleep.

Residents of the Tenderloin spent most of their time trying to eke out a living in any one of various trades, including the sex trade. For the record, my mother was not part of the sex trade. I may have been illegitimate, but I know with certainty that my mother was not that "kind" of a woman. To the best of my knowledge, she wasn't gay, either.

My mother worked hard to earn a meager living for the two of us. She was a cleaning lady. She cleaned bars. She cleaned them after the last round was drunk by drunks. My mother worked nights and slept all day. This meant I got the bed all to myself every night except Sunday. Sunday was her day off. So when she got home from her job early Sunday morning, she usually slept around the clock until Monday afternoon. Then she prepared herself to set off for duty to scrub the crud, crap, and corruption left behind by boozers. Sunday nights I slept on the floor.

I may know what kind of woman my mother wasn't, but to this day, I really don't know what kind of woman she was. I know less about my father. My Aunt Edna told me I was named after him. But when I asked my mother, she claimed otherwise. Instead, she said I was named to honor two important men of history. She gave me Marcus as my first name to honor a Roman emperor, and Plato as my middle name to honor a Greek philosopher. Of all the famous people in history, why did she choose those two? Why couldn't she have picked the name of an American president such as John Fitzgerald Kennedy or a famous singer such as Elvis Presley? When I was born, both names were more popular and relevant in the 1960s than mine. It would have been so great to be able to introduce myself as Elvis Fitzgerald Hanlon rather than Marcus Plato Hanlon. Despite her claims, I suspect she was influenced by my father when she chose my name. So I believed my Aunt Edna more than I believed my mother. I believe she picked my first and middle names to reflect my father's heritage. The proof, as they say, is in the pudding.

Both my mother and Aunt Edna had ginger hair and freckles. They were both about five feet six inches tall and slender. By contrast, my hair is black and my skin is swarthy. I was and have always been short and dumpy. I look nothing like the Hanlon sisters. So I believe my father was Italian, Greek, or a combination of both. However, because North Beach is predominately Italian, I believe that I am too. When people ask about my heritage, I tell them I am Italian and Irish. No one has ever argued with me, although they always ask me from which part of Italy my family came. I tell them Sicily. When they press me for more details, I tell them Catania. To me, this story sounds good. It must also sound plausible, because no one has ever asked me for more information.

Although my mother seldom mentioned my father, I believe he must have been quite a guy for two reasons: one, because he got her to have sex with him; and two, because she never dated anyone else her entire life, as far as I know. I am not sure if it's because my father was so great or if it's because he was so rotten that he put her off men forever.

When I was little, I thought my father must be important. In response to my incessant interest in him, my mother would always say "Jesus H. Christ, would you stop with all the questions about your father?" For many years, I thought my father's name was actually

Jesus Christ. That he was named after someone so important made him seem even more important to me. Yet I always wondered what the "H" stood for. Was my father's middle name Howard, Harold, Herman, or something else? In my dreams, the "H" always stood for Hubert, after Vice President Hubert Humphrey. When I was six years old, I dreamed big and believed my dreams could come true. When I saw Hubert Humphrey on television, I thought he would be a really good dad. In 1968, I wrote Mr. Humphrey a letter to see if he had time to be my dad. Like my real father, I didn't hear from him, either.

Chapter 3
Spotless

I may have grown up without a dad, but I grew up with a mother.
Rita Marie Hanlon was a woman of few words. She seldom offered
any words of endearment. In her own way, I know she cared for me.
After all, she could have taken the easy way out and aborted me.
It would have posed a great risk, but in the Tenderloin anything,
including abortion, was possible. She could have given me up for
adoption. It would have posed no risk and was equally possible. She
didn't abort me. She didn't give me up. I'm sure these were difficult
decisions for her to make, especially after her parents disowned her.
Instead, she found a job and a place for us to live. For the rest of her
life, she lived in the same two-room apartment in the same building
on Hyde Street.

As I mentioned before, my mother was a cleaning lady. To me she
wasn't cleaning lady; she was a lady who happened to clean. Rita
Marie Hanlon may not have lived on Nob Hill, but she tried to be
just as much a lady as any of the society matrons who did live there.
My mother was always polite. She expected no less from me.

When I was a few years old, my mother would sing a song to me
called "Magic Words." According to the song, the magic words were
"please" and "thank you." These "little magic" words were among the
first I learned. I still am not sure why they are called magic words. At
no time did they help me pull a rabbit out of a hat or turn a copper
penny into a silver dollar. Despite what my mother sang to me, they
didn't open any doors with ease. I wished those little words had been
magical, not only for me, but also for my mother. Still, she insisted
I always use "please" and "thank you." She taught me other words.

They were polite words such as "yes, sir"; "no, sir"; "yes, ma'am"; and "no, ma'am." Responses such as "yep" and "nope" didn't have a place in our home. She told me children should be seen and not heard. She also often said what happened within our apartment must stay within our apartment.

Even though I may have known magic and other polite words, none of them took me beyond our apartment or gained me any greater entry into doors in the Tenderloin. As it turns out, my mother need not have worried. I was neither heard nor seen. And she need not have worried about whatever happened in our apartment, either. Nothing happened. So all stayed behind. After all, what would I have told? Who would I have told? Who would have listened?

My mother's voice was different. When she spoke, which wasn't often, her voice was soft but low. To me, she sounded a lot like Lauren Bacall. When she sang, her voice was also soft and low. To me, she sounded like Patty Paige. Unfortunately, she seldom spoke or sang to me or to anyone else. She kept to herself and spoke mainly to the other voices she alone could hear. My mother spoke to many voices. She had at least seven voices that I can remember. It seemed she had one for every day of the week. Her Saturday voice was best, and her Monday voice was the worst. I don't know why. My best guess is Saturday marked the end of her work week and a chance for rest. Monday marked the beginning another work week and no chance of rest. I never asked her about the voices. Her conversations with them seemed so private and so intimate that I didn't want to interrupt. I was also sure she wouldn't answer me if I did ask about them.

It's difficult for me now to remember everything about my mother and how I grew up in the Tenderloin. To me, memories are tricky things. I suspect I am no different from anyone else. I can easily remember really good times and really bad times. But I have trouble remembering the inbetween times. Ordinary day-to-day activities are difficult to remember. By their very nature, they are common, mundane, and don't stand out, so they are easy to forget. Just the same, I believe most of us crave ordinary, commonplace days.

I admire people who keep daily diaries or journals. What do they record? Do they just write down the highs and the lows? Or do they also memorialize the mundane? What I mean is, do people write down what they ate for breakfast, or do they save their journal pages for more important activities such as visits to the theater or the opera? I have to rely on what memories remain of my mother, my Aunt Edna, and everything else. Sadly, most events of my life were so ordinary that it's difficult for me to recall them. None were worthy enough to write down.

I do remember my mother always seemed old to me. It's ironic, because she was only seventeen when I was born. When you're five or six, all adults, even teenagers, seem old. When I was six, my mother was twenty-three. She was young by any standards. Despite her youth, my mother looked old to me then. In retrospect, I suspect she didn't look old as much as she looked worn out. But as a child, I couldn't tell the difference. I know now that hard work took a toll on my mother's appearance. I have no recollection of her standing straight or walking smartly down the street. Her shoulders were always curled forward. She walked slowly. Her feet seemed to drag behind her as if she wore cinder blocks instead of shoes.

My mother and I didn't have much, but we always had a roof over our heads. I never went hungry. I don't know if my mother went hungry or not, because I don't remember seeing her eat except on special days like Thanksgiving, Christmas, or Easter. My clothes were always clean and well-pressed. The same can't be said for everyone who has ever called the Tenderloin home. If I ever felt short changed, it was because, except for my sidewalk spots, I had no playmates.

During the 1960s, I knew of no children who called the Tenderloin home.

My mother and I had each other. And we had Aunt Edna. There were three of us, which can't be said for others who lived in our neighborhood. A city, even San Francisco, can be a lonely place to live. I am grateful I was not alone. I had my mother and my Aunt Edna.

Chapter 4
Spotlight

My Aunt Edna was something else. She was different from my mother. While my mother seemed colorless, Aunt Edna was the opposite. When Aunt Edna walked into a room, it was like opening a large new box of crayons. She was colorful. She wore rouge, lipstick, and nice clothes. My mother always said Aunt Edna wore her clothes too tight, but Aunt Edna always looked good to me. Other guys liked how she looked, too. When Aunt Edna strutted down the Tenderloin streets, men stepped aside and whistled.

Aunt Edna liked to wear lots of jewelry. When other women would wear one bracelet, Aunt Edna would wear five or six. They jingled when she walked or raised her arm to wave at someone she knew. Aunt Edna seemed to know everyone, mostly men. She also carried a big handbag. It often contained treats for me such as a lollipop or Bazooka chewing gum. My favorite handbag was her black shiny one. I remember how it used to sparkle in the sun when she walked down Hyde Street on the way to our apartment.

Long before Jacqueline Kennedy became famous for hiding her eyes behind big black sunglasses, Aunt Edna sported large white ones. They had rhinestones in the upper right- and left-hand corners. They shimmered like real diamonds. She was glamorous. I don't remember her being beautiful in a *Vogue* fashion magazine sense. She was beautiful in a *National Enquirer* tabloid newspaper sense. Aunt Edna was like a movie star to me.

Everyone should have an Aunt Edna. When she spoke to me, Aunt Edna always made me believe I was not only the most important person in the room, but also the most important person on Earth. Aunt Edna made me feel special every time I saw her, which was about once a week as long as she and my mother were on speaking terms. From time to time, they would argue. Their arguments would escalate. They were always about the same thing: religion. The extent of their anger depended on how much beer they consumed.

My mother was Roman Catholic. She believed and told anyone who would listen that the Roman Catholic Church was the "only true church in all of Christendom." Aunt Edna would not listen. She held different beliefs. I don't know what religion my Aunt Edna chose to follow, but I do know my mother also believed Aunt Edna was going straight to hell because of it. Although my mother was a woman of few words, she had lots to say about my Aunt Edna's religion. After they each drank three beers, I can remember my mother called it "half-assed and half baked." After they drank five beers, I cannot and will not repeat what else my mother said. Suffice to say, those words usually led to a fight that exceeded all the others. Every time, it was punctuated by the slam of the door as my Aunt Edna left in disgust and cried out, "I won't darken your door again!"

As a youngster, I couldn't believe Aunt Edna could darken our door. I believed she brought in lots of light and color. I couldn't understand why my mother got so upset about something she seldom practiced anyway. As far as I know, Aunt Edna was still a Christian, which is what should have mattered. Of course, my mother saw things differently, and she insisted I see things her way, too. And I did see things her way until I moved out on my own.

Meanwhile, I managed to learn a little about Aunt Edna's religion. Instead of church on Sunday, she went on Saturday. Personally, I liked the idea of going to church on Saturday. I thought, why not get it out of the way early? Aunt Edna must have been serious about her religion because she didn't wear any makeup or jewelry when she went to her church. She made great sacrifices for her religion every week. My mother didn't seem to make any sacrifices for hers. She didn't have to give up makeup or jewelry because she didn't wear any. Unlike Aunt Edna, I don't remember my mother going to church regularly, either. My mother went three times a year: Christmas Day, Ash Wednesday, and Easter Sunday.

From time to time, Aunt Edna would have a boyfriend. Some were more serious than others. I could always tell when a boyfriend held a special place in her heart. Aunt Edna would ask me to call him "uncle." Over twenty years, I probably had at least twenty uncles. They came in all shapes, ages, and sizes. When Aunt Edna held a special place in an uncle's heart, he would give me fifty cents to go away and leave them alone. Over fifteen years, I made enough to buy tickets to the movies was well as popcorn and sodas. If I was lucky, Aunt Edna and her latest "uncle" might take me to see a movie and buy the snacks. Then I would get to keep whatever money this latest "uncle" gave me.

I liked to sit close to the movie screen, especially for epic movies such as *Spartacus* or *Ben Hur*. As far as I was concerned, all the action was best seen from a seat in the front row. As far as Aunt Edna and her latest boyfriend were concerned, all the action could be found in the last row of the loge. Maybe it had something to do with Aunt Edna's religion that made her want to sit so far away. Or, maybe she saw the movie differently from her vantage point. Regardless, I had great times with my Aunt Edna. She didn't darken doors; she opened up new ones for me.

The doors I remember best are the ones that opened up to the movies. In the 1960s and 1970s, movie theaters were different than they are now. Movie theaters such as the Tower, St. Francis, and Castro had one large screen on which they showed the same movie over and over again during its run. Today, one movie theater may have sixteen screens or more. When I was young, a movie's run could be as long as two or three months if it was popular.

On Saturdays, Aunt Edna would buy our tickets from the attendant at the booth, which was usually out front and apart from the main theater entrance. Then we would stand in line to wait for our turn to go in for the next show. From time to time, the head usher would ensure we stood in an orderly fashion—no more than two abreast—so as not to block the sidewalk. I assumed he was the head usher because he usually wore a blazer, whereas the other ushers simply wore white shirts, bow ties, and sometimes vests.

I remember one head usher in particular. He had straight black hair parted on the side. His part was perfect. I am sure he used a straight edge to get it so even. Not one hair on his head was out of place. His hair was slick and looked unnatural. I suspect he may have used a product called Brylcreem. The advertisements for Brylcreem used to say, "A little dab'll do ya!" Either this usher didn't see the advertisement or he thought four large dabs would do him. He was wrong. His hair looked as if it were shellacked. His sideburns were an art unto themselves. I don't know how he achieved such perfect symmetry on either side of his face. He must have used a masterful combination of comb, scissors, and tweezers, and perhaps even masking tape and a carpenter's level.

After we made it through the front doors and had our tickets ripped in half by the attendant, Aunt Edna and I headed to the concession stand. As a boy, I never understood why it was called a concession stand. Who conceded what and to whom? All I remember is Aunt Edna paid at least three times the market rate for a bag of popcorn and a soda. Years later, I learned the movie theaters granted rights to sell snacks to outside providers. Based on what we paid for popcorn, candy, and sodas, those rights were expensive. Nonetheless, I couldn't imagine watching a movie without popcorn. I still can't.

I like a little salt and lots of butter on my popcorn. Movie theater popcorn butter is different from any I have ever seen for sale at any supermarket. First of all, movie butter is always runny, even if the theater is cold. Supermarket butter is never runny, even if it's served at room temperature. So I always wondered if the butter is real at the movie theater.

Movie butter is always pumped onto the popcorn. The amount you receive depends both on wrist action and whether butter is added after each shovel of popcorn is loaded into the bag. I have never seen anyone measure how much butter goes onto the popcorn in each bag. I believe a large bag should get more butter than the medium. But if you watch the attendant, each bag usually gets three pumps, regardless of bag size. To compensate, I always asked for extra butter. Even then, there was no guarantee my popcorn tasted buttery. It seems to me if concession owners were interested in happy customers and quality control, they would measure butter better.

Between uncles and movies, and before she sat for a few beers with my mother, Aunt Edna would often take me to different places after her Saturday church service. From the Tenderloin, we walked to many places. I think it was during those walks I first noticed sidewalk spots.

In the Tenderloin, we didn't drive to places we wanted to see. No one I knew owned a car. Instead, we relied on public transportation or what we referred to as old-fashioned shoe leather to get us where we wanted to go. Of course, the idea of anyone in my neighborhood owning leather-soled shoes is laughable. In the Tenderloin, most shoe soles were made of neoprene, not leather. To make those soles last longer, it was customary to nail half-moon shaped metal cleats on the heels and toes. A busy street could sound like a bad tap dance audition. When the neoprene became thin, a cardboard insole could make shoes a little more comfortable and make them last a little while longer.

As a kid, I wore either PF Flyers or Converse high tops. The tops were made of black canvas and the soles were made of white rubber. I tied them up with white laces. I had one pair of brown hard-soled shoes with brown laces my mother said were reserved for church and special events. I wore them to church. I have no recollection of any special events. The days with Aunt Edna were always special to me, but they were not special enough for my mother. She wouldn't let me wear my brown hard-soled shoes when I went out with Aunt Edna. As a result, I usually outgrew my hard-soled shoes before they were scuffed.

Chapter 5
Walks

My life didn't really begin until I started school. I remember my first day of kindergarten as if it were yesterday. I traded a room barely big enough for one child for a room big enough to hold thirty children who, except for the teacher, all happened to be my age. Until my first day at school, my playground had been the sidewalk between our apartment and Hyde Street. My sidewalk spots kept me company during the days I didn't see Aunt Edna. No other children showed up to play.

In the 1960s, the Tenderloin was not a place for children. There were no parks, and there was no school until the 1990s. Any children from the Tenderloin went to any school that would take them. In the 1970s, some children went to school on Treasure Island. It wasn't an option for me. I was going to school in North Beach. It's where my mother and Aunt Edna went to school, so I went there, too.

School gave me an education and most of my lifelong friends. I made most of my friendships in kindergarten. I made a few other friends as I passed through first through eighth grades. Although I met lots of new students when I got into high school, I made no new lifelong friends as I had in elementary school.

Before I started school, any supervision that came to me while my mother slept or worked came from passersby who didn't hesitate to tell me what to do and how to do it. However, this kind of supervision was based on what was better for them, not for me. On my first day, I knew my kindergarten classroom was going to be based on what was best for me.

My mother walked with me on my first day to show me the way to school. She also walked with me at the end of my first day to show me the way home. It was a long walk for her and for me. At age five, my legs were shorter than hers. A forty-block walk is a long way for anyone. But it was tougher for my mother, not only because she had to come back for me at the end of my first school day, but she also had to go to work after. Thankfully, I could remember the way by memory because my mother never walked me to or from school again. It's just as well. It was during those walks that I found new sidewalk spots and became serious about my collection.

My first day of school was special. I guess it must have been special for my mother, too, because she let me wear my brown hard-soled shoes. She also bought me a new shirt and pants—not jeans, but pants. I knew my first day of school was a special day for my Aunt Edna also, because she stopped by to take my photograph.

What can I say about my school? Like all cities' elementary schools, it was utilitarian in design and practical in application. I have always suspected that school boards have one set of architectural plans that they use from city to city and state to state. All schools look the same. I can imagine some baldheaded stuffy school superintendent peering over his wire-rimmed glasses saying, "Students are there to learn, not to be inspired."

Like other city schools, our playground was asphalt except where the pavement had worn away and left behind a sorry mixture of gravel and dirt. No playground surface was fun to fall on. If I didn't scrape my elbows, I was certain to graze the palms of my hands or fray the knees of my trousers.

After nine years of elementary school, just three teachers stand out in my memory. The first is Miss O'Hara. She introduced herself to us on my first day of kindergarten. This was also the first time I had heard a woman refer to herself as "Miss." I wondered what she had missed.

Miss O'Hara was tall and stately and had blonde hair. She always wore colorful sweater sets to go with her pleated plaid skirts. She filled out her sweaters in a different way than either my mother or my Aunt Edna. Miss O'Hara looked as if she had inserted two pointed Dixie Cup cones where her breasts should have been. Her breasts looked unnatural. One day I discovered they were when she bumped into the wall by the cloakroom. All of a sudden, those horizontal pyramids turned into a couple of sunken volcanoes. The entire class chuckled. She ignored us and pretended nothing happened. Despite this fall from grace, Miss O'Hara was, in my estimation, beautiful.

Miss O'Hara also smelled nice. Later, I found out she wore Old Yardley. I wondered why someone so young and so pretty would wear something described as old. Anything old should have been reserved for someone old like my second grade teacher, Mrs. Sturgess.

Mrs. Sturgess was old. She looked as if she were over one hundred years old. Of course, to a seven-year-old kid, even twenty-two looks old. But Mrs. Sturgess was old. I can't believe she was ever a "Miss" like Miss O'Hara. I knew Mrs. Sturgess was married; otherwise, why would she refer to herself as "Mrs."? But she confused me. Time and time again, she would refer to her "late husband." It was a long time before I figured out he wasn't tardy; he was dead.

Mrs. Sturgess had lots of wrinkles. Her face and hands were wrinkled. She was average height, was plump, and had grey hair. Her boobs were nothing like Miss O'Hara's. Instead of being pointy, they were like balloons. I wished she could have worn something stronger to hold them up. Throughout the day, she either pulled them up with the straps of her brassiere or pushed them up with her hands as if they weighed too much for her shoulders. It seemed that Mrs. Sturgess pulled and pushed her boobs at least a hundred times a day.

Mrs. Sturgess often dabbed her nose with a tissue and then tucked it into the top of her dress between her boobs. For a long while, I thought her boobs might collapse under the additional weight of tissues. They didn't. I never saw them put to the cloakroom wall test, either. If she had bumped into the cloakroom or any other wall, I am confident her boobs would have bounced back, no matter how many tissues she had stuffed down the front of her dress.

Because she was old, I always wondered why Mrs. Sturgess didn't wear Old Yardley. Don't get me wrong. Mrs. Sturgess smelled nice. She smelled like Camay soap. She smelled like my Aunt Edna, which made her okay in my book.

Despite their physical differences, Miss O'Hara and Mrs. Sturgess were good teachers. They made me look forward to school every day. I learned a lot from them. I learned how to write my name and use times tables, among many other subjects. They took time to explain things in words and ways I could understand. They made me want to be a better in all ways except for their boobs. I didn't want boobs, but I wanted to learn. I wanted to grow up and be a teacher like them until I encountered my eighth grade teacher, Miss Rafferty.

Between Mrs. Sturgess in the second grade and Miss Rafferty in the eighth grade, I had five other teachers for the third, fourth, fifth, sixth, and seventh grades. These teachers were unmemorable. All were women. I guess you would call them average age. They were also average teachers. They had their idiosyncrasies. For example, Mrs. Bannister of the sixth grade wore weird eye glasses. They were cut in half and had no tops. When they weren't perched on the end of her nose, they dangled from a chain around her neck. I always wondered why she didn't buy entire glasses rather than just a half portion. Maybe they were cheaper.

I would have given anything to have a man for a teacher. But the four men in our school didn't teach. Two of the men were custodians. The third man was the vice principal, and the fourth was the principal.

I liked the custodians. Their names, Henry and Frank, were sewn on the pockets of the dark blue shirts. They took care of our school. They made sure, among many other things, that our wooden floors shone, our drinking fountains worked, and our toilets flushed. They also looked after our school's exterior. While they never repaired the playground, they made sure the sidewalk out front was kept clear. One time I even saw Frank try to take the spots off. He struggled, but nothing he did could make them come off. Although the job seemed to frustrate him, as a protector of sidewalk spots, it made me happy.

We could always tell where Henry and Frank were or where they were going. It wasn't the sound of their shoes but the sounds their keys made when they walked. I have never seen anyone carry as many keys as Henry and Frank. Their keys were on big metal rings attached to chains that hung from belt loops of their dark blue pants. In addition to the dark blue shirts and pants, Henry and Frank wore black boots with thick rubber soles. I liked how they looked and thought it would be fun to be a custodian when I grew up. I wondered if I would qualify to have my name on my shirt.

The principal and the vice principal didn't wear anything as attractive as our custodians. Our principal, Mr. Charles, always wore a grey suit. Our vice principal, Mr. Rudnick, always wore a brown suit. Both were as colorless as their suits. Both were unmemorable.

How do I describe my eighth grade teacher, Miss Rafferty? She was a woman of indeterminate age. She wasn't as young as Miss O'Hara. She seemed older than Mrs. Bannister, but not as old as Mrs. Sturgess. I guessed she was somewhat old.

It didn't take me long to figure out why she was a "Miss" and not a "Mrs." Miss Rafferty was as broad as she was high. She was short and squat and had messy brown hair. To this day, I think of her as a fuzzy-haired bowling ball. As to her boobs, I have no idea where she hid them. They lurked somewhere in the folds of her torso.

Miss Rafferty was so short that she couldn't pull down the map at the front of the classroom. She had to use a stick with a hook to grasp the chrome ring on the end of the map. Even with the stick, it was still a bit of a stretch for her. When she stretched, her dress would lift up enough for us to see the tops of her nylon stockings, which she knotted to keep them up. Thankfully, we were not treated to anything higher. As it was, her knees were sights to behold. From behind, the backs of knees looked like bags of boulders. Unlike Miss O'Hara and Mrs. Sturgess, Miss Rafferty smelled, but not like Old Yardley or Camay. She stunk.

Most of the time, Miss Rafferty smelled like urine. This wasn't a figment of my imagination. The whole class noticed it, too. When she was especially ripe, we could hardly wait for recess to begin. Once we were outdoors, we could hardly wait to talk about the stench. A few of the girls in my class tried to come up with ways to overcome her smell, such as perfumed cream on our noses. The guys had no interest in scented creams. Short of Air Wick in class, we were doomed to endure Miss Rafferty's smell from September until June.

All of us dreaded any time we were called to the front of the class. Our fear wasn't because we had to face the class, which was tough enough, but because we had to stand close to her. Her smell overpowered us. We equally dreaded any time she decided to walk down the aisles between our desks. We prayed she wouldn't stop beside us. After all, there's only so long a guy can hold his breath until his face turns red. We tried breathing through our mouths, but it didn't work. Her smell eventually made it to the backs of our throats and made us cough.

All the students knew about her. If she smelled in our classroom, we knew she had to smell in the teachers' lounge, too. We always wondered why one of her colleagues, such as Miss O'Hara or Mrs. Sturgess, didn't speak to her about it. Maybe, like us, they were overcome. After a while, we began to believe Miss Rafferty was an eighth grade rite of passage. If we could endure her smell, we could go to high school.

If her body odor wasn't enough, Miss Rafferty had another issue that was equally offensive. We found out about this issue early in the school year. What's worse, we also found out she not only knew about it, but she didn't care. When Miss Rafferty bent over a desk to check a student's work, she regularly passed gas. Simply stated, she farted, and she farted loudly. Miss Rafferty added another bad smell to her odor repertoire.

The first time we heard the unmistakable noise, we all raised our heads and looked around in amazement. No one could believe it actually happened. Nobody said a word or made a move. The second, time, we also raised our heads in disbelief. This time, though, we knew it actually happened. Thirty-eight eighth graders can't be fooled. We had heard it with our own ears. A few looked around to see to see if they could find the culprit. A few others snickered. But, once again, no one said a word or made a move. The third time, as they say, was the charm.

We discovered it was Miss Rafferty who was the deadly deed doer. We raised our heads and laughed out loud. What surprised us even more was Miss Rafferty's response. She stood up straight, turned toward the entire class, and said, "What did you expect, chimes?" We were nonplussed. She made no excuses. She made no apologies. Instead, she left a legacy no teacher before her or after her left behind. Miss Rafferty made me yearn for a whiff of Miss O'Hara's Old Yardley or Mrs. Sturgess' Camay.

Although some of my elementary school teachers made impressions, for better or worse, my friends made greater impressions on me.

Chapter 6
Soft Spots

While I knew my way to school, it took me a while to find my way in kindergarten. As an only child and one who lived in a neighborhood without other children, I had spent no time with kids my own age. To find myself in the company of so many children excited and frightened me. The thought of new friends excited me. The thought of no friends frightened me. As it turned out, I didn't have to worry.

My fears evaporated on the second day of school. A boy came up to me and said, "Hey, kid, what's your name?"

"Marcus Plato Hanlon," I said.

"What kind of name is that?"

I stood there dumbfounded. I couldn't think of a response. My fears returned.

"What's the matter, cat got your tongue?"

Again, I just stood there with a blank look on my face and wondered what kind of cats get tongues. I couldn't think of anything to say. Even if I could have come up with something, I was too bowled over by his brashness for any words to come out.

I was grateful this boy was undeterred by my stunned silence. He said, "My name is Arthur Lefkowitz, but everyone calls me Nobby. You can call me Nobby, too."

In just a few moments, I made a friend. Before we could go any further in this relationship, our teacher called the class to attention. I would have to wait until recess to learn more about Nobby. I hoped I hadn't put him off.

I could hardly wait for the morning recess bell to ring. As instructed, we lined up in a single file. We were silent as we exited our classroom in an orderly fashion until we reached the school's exit doors. Once we were outside those doors, classroom order made way for confusion. Some kids ran to play catch, some to pay tag, and others to play marbles. Some kids, especially the girls, formed little groups. One group of girls just stood around and talked. Another group played a game that was unknown to me. I learned this game was called "skipping."

Nobby was ahead of me in line. I expected him to run off with other guys. I didn't expect to see him during recess. So I was surprised to find he had waited for me just outside the door. To the left of Nobby stood another boy. He was different from Nobby and from me. Nobby introduced him and called him Rusty. Finally, I worked up enough courage to speak. I asked Nobby why he was called Nobby rather than Arthur. Nobby explained his brothers gave him the nickname because he was so skinny.

"Why didn't they call you Skinny instead of Nobby?" I asked.

"Because my older brother, Frederick, is called Skinny, that's why. My bones stick out everywhere. That's why they call me Nobby."

"My real name isn't Rusty, either. My real name is Charles," the other boy said.

Even Nobby was surprised. "I thought your first name was Russell!" exclaimed Nobby. "Why do they call you Rusty then?"

"Look at my hair," said Rusty. "It's the color of rust."

That was the day I made two new friends. The three of us spent every recess together from kindergarten though eighth grade. From time to

time, others would join our trio and leave, but the three of us stayed
and played together.

A couple of weeks later, Nobby started calling me Playdough. "That's
what we're gonna call ya from now on," he said.

"Why Playdough?" I asked.

"It sounds sorta like your name Plato. Get it?" said Nobby. I got it all
right. By the look on my face, Nobby could tell I wasn't happy about
it. "You gotta have a nickname to fit in. It's a good thing. Think of it
this way. We care enough to think of something else to call you other
than your real name. We could have called you Chubby, like Marshall
Hershberg over there. Or we could have called you Piggy, like Jimmy
Jameson. But we don't want to be mean to you. You're an okay guy, so
we came up with a good name. Everybody likes Playdough."

I accepted the inevitable and expressed great relief Nobby hadn't used
Marcus as his inspiration. If he had, I am sure Nobby would have
come up with Mucus as my nickname. Mucus would have been too
much to bear.

Nobby came up with what he thought were good nicknames for
everyone he liked. Interestingly, he had no nicknames for people
about whom he was ambivalent. His nicknames for people he didn't
like bordered on being cruel. Yet Chubby Hershberg and Piggy
Jameson didn't seem to mind. They were happy just to be noticed by
guys like Nobby. As a result, they put up with whatever he deigned
to call them. You see, Nobby was a popular guy. He told us so. We
believed him, and so did many of the other kids.

Nobby always called Mary Ellen Henderson by her real name,
although he often referred to her as a brown-noser because she was
so smart and was always the first to put up her hand in class. Once,
I asked him why he didn't call her Browner. Nobby said, "What
would be the point? She's got red hair, too. I could call her Red. But

she has her nose stuck so far in the air, she doesn't even pay attention to anything guys like me say to her." Nobby, even as a five-year-old, had an uncanny sense about people. He always seemed to know how far he could push without getting punched. I admired his self-assuredness.

As I look back on our school days together, I believe Nobby should have been a psychiatrist. Just as he could read a room and figure out how to fit in, he could read people and know how to get them to like him. When Nobby listened, he made us feel important, at least to him anyway. Everyone likes to feel important. I did. I hung onto Nobby like a barnacle on the bottom of a boat. Although we never talked about it, I sensed Rusty felt the same way about Nobby as I did.

Like me, Rusty had no brothers or sisters. Just as I looked for friends, I suspected Rusty looked for them, too. Nobby offered friendship to both of us. He also became the glue that held us together. Unlike Rusty and me, Nobby had brothers and sisters. He had two older brothers and two younger brothers. He also had an older sister and a younger sister. Nobby was in the middle of a large family.

Like us, Nobby's family didn't have any money. We could tell by the way he dressed. Nobby didn't start the school year in new pants, shirt, and shoes. He wore hand-me-downs from his older brothers. We could see the lines on his pants where the cuffs had gone up and down based on his brothers' rates of growth. We could also see the patches on his knees.

Because he came from a large family, I figured Nobby lived in a larger apartment than I did. It had to be bigger to accommodate nine people. Many years later, when we were both in our teens, Nobby asked me over to his place in North Beach while his parents were away. His apartment was bigger than the one my mother and I lived in. It had two bedrooms and one bathroom. His mother and father slept in one bedroom, Nobby and his brothers slept in the second bedroom, and his sisters slept on a pull-out couch in the living room. Nobby's apartment was clean, neat, and tidy, which surprised me considering how many people shared the space. I don't know how they managed in such a small space, but they did in the same way my mother and I did. Nobby may not have been dressed in new clothes, but he always had clean ones.

Rusty told us he and his father lived with his grandmother. He didn't offer to say where, and he didn't volunteer any more information when asked. He simply said he lived with his grandmother as if we should know where it was. Rusty always came to school in clean clothes, although he didn't seem to have many choices in any given school year. We always saw him in one of two green plaid shirts or one of two pairs of pants, khaki or navy. He always wore heavy laceup leather boots. At the start of the school year, the leather had a nice medium brown patina and the soles were beige. I used to think I would like a pair, too. By the end of the school year, the leather on the toes had peeled away, the laces had knots to hold them together, the soles had tuned dark, and the tread on the bottom was non-existent. By then, I wasn't so keen on them. I don't know what Rusty wore during summer vacations—maybe no shoes at all. However, come September and our first day of school, he always had a new pair of boots.

As I became more comfortable with the daily routine of school, I started to gain confidence, but in front of the class, I was always tongue-tied. I never got over it. However, I became more vocal during recess in front of my friends, Nobby and Rusty. "Why don't we get a rope and try skipping?" I asked the guys one day.

"That's a girls' game!" Nobby exclaimed. I don't know why he called it a girls' game, but I knew enough not to argue with him.

Nobby suggested we should try marbles. "Now that's a guy's game!" he declared. As much as I wanted to play marbles, I had a problem—I had no marbles. I also didn't know where I could get some. When one is in the first grade, the idea of a marble collection is formidable.

While I contemplated my dilemma, Rusty spoke. "I don't have any marbles, and I don't know where to get any."

As always, Nobby had all the answers. "You go to the toy section in Woolworth's. They've got bags of them in all kinds of colors and sizes."

Rusty shook his head and said, "But I don't have any money." He wasn't alone. I didn't have any money, either. It seemed that marbles were out of reach and we would have to be content to play tag or toss a ball. I was wrong.

Nobby was undeterred. "I don't let a little thing like no money get in my way. I'll borrow a few from each of my brothers, and then I'll win more when I play the other guys during recess."

Rusty looked at me, and I looked back at him. We shrugged our shoulders. We had no brothers from whom we could borrow anything, much less marbles. Once again, Nobby was out of our league. We would stand by and support him. Hopefully, we could share in his gains and learn something, too.

We didn't have to wait long. The very next day, Nobby showed us a handful of marbles he got from his brothers. He was ready to make his fortune.

"Have you ever played this game before?" I asked.

"Of course," Nobby answered. "What kind of moron do you think I am? I play with my brothers all the time. They're champions, and they've taught me all their tricks."

"What kinds of tricks?" asked Rusty.

44

Nobby stuck out his chin and said, "The most important trick is to watch carefully and find out who plays the game worst. Then, you take him on first." We could hardly wait for recess.

The bell rang and we ran out to the playground. We could hardly wait for the marble games to begin. Nobby didn't jump right in and play. Instead, he watched, just as he said he would. He watched all recess.

"When are you going to play?" asked Rusty.

"Tomorrow," said Nobby. "It's taken me all recess to figure out who I can beat."

The next day came. Once again, we could hardly wait until Nobby clobbered his competition and came away with lots of marbles. Rusty and I were excited. We would stand on the sidelines, like cheerleaders, and watch as Nobby creamed his opponents. Today, however, we were disappointed. Nobby didn't bring any marbles with him to school.

"What happened?" Rusty and I asked in unison.

"My brothers needed all their marbles today. I'll try to play tomorrow. The competition isn't going anywhere."

Another day came. Still, Nobby had no marbles. Then another day, and no marbles. Finally, after a whole week went by, Nobby came to school with marbles. I'd like to say our excitement grew as each day passed, but it didn't. After four days, we began to wonder if we would ever see a showdown between Nobby and his weakest opponent. Nobby referred to this guy as either "the chump" or "the pigeon." We had no idea what his name was. We did know he was in the first grade, which made him more formidable than any kid from kindergarten.

The bell rang, and we ran out to the playground again. We couldn't wait for the marble games to begin. Nobby sauntered over toward the area where his chump usually played. The chump stood there and held a large bag of marbles in his right hand. He had far more marbles than Nobby had in his pockets. And the chump carried his marbles in a leather bag with a leather lace drawstring. He looked like a professional marble player. We didn't know if the chump had won them or bought them. If he won them, he wasn't going to be the chump Nobby thought he was.

The marbles were lined up. For the first game, the winner got to keep all the marbles to the left of the marble he hit. Nobby rolled his shooter. He aimed for the last marble at the right end of the line. He missed. Then the chump rolled his shooter. He also aimed for the last marble at the right end of the line. He missed. Next time, Nobby aimed more to the center. He made a hit and captured six marbles in the line. They played another match and another. Nobby was winning every game. Then the bell rang. Recess ended, and the games stopped.

Nobby came away with seventeen additional marbles—not a bad haul for someone who didn't own any marbles of his own.

"See ya, kid," said the chump. Apparently, he harbored no hard feelings over his loss.

Nobby said, "See ya!" As far as we knew, that was that. However, once outside the view of the chump, Nobby could barely contain his excitement. "I did it! I did it!" Nobby cried. "I gambled and I won!" Who knew just how prophetic his claim would be.

Today, at least, Nobby was a winner. He could keep his seventeen marbles and return the remainder to his brothers who, we found out later, had no idea Nobby had borrowed them. It was a day for us to celebrate. But it was also a day that marked the start of Nobby's pattern of risky behavior that Rusty and I watched from the sidelines.

Nobby had his marbles, and I had my sidewalk spots. I discovered more and more spots as I walked to and from school. While they may have been in public places, they were private spots to me. I never talked about my spots to anyone. Mine was a private collection. They were too important to me to share. Their constancy consoled me. I didn't know what Rusty had to console himself. He never talked about his life after school. When we reached the fourth grade, I learned more about my friend Rusty.

Chapter 7
Walk Away

Soon after we started the fourth grade, Rusty surprised me. He told me he was turning ten and asked if I wanted to come to his place to help him celebrate his birthday. I don't know why Rusty asked me and not Nobby. After all, it was Nobby who introduced me to Rusty, but I didn't ask why. I simply thanked him and said I would have to ask my mother if it was okay to follow him home after school for his birthday dinner.

My mother gave her permission, and then she surprised me. She asked what I wanted to give Rusty for his birthday. The thought of a gift hadn't crossed my mind. This was the first birthday party to which I had ever been invited. I didn't know anything about birthday protocol. So I suggested a game.

Who knows when my mother found the time or the money, but a couple of days later she showed me what she had purchased for Rusty, a game called "Battleship." I was impressed she had come through with a gift. It was one I would have liked to receive. When I tried to thank her, she just looked away and said, "Okay, okay, it's no big deal. I'll wrap it later." But it was a big deal. It wasn't that the gift might impress Rusty, although I hoped it would. Instead it was that, for this occasion, my mother impressed me in an unexpected way. Not only had she bought a great gift, but she was going to wrap it, too. I don't know what voices in her head had spoken to her over those few days, but I hoped they would stick around.

Tuesday rolled around. My mother had wrapped the gift and put it in a brown paper shopping bag with handles so it was easier to carry. I was grateful for this, too, because I didn't want to attract any attention once I got to school, especially from Nobby. I needn't have worried. As usual, no one noticed me or the bag. Once I was in the classroom, I slid it into my desk.

At the end of the school day, Rusty and I dawdled until the others were well ahead of us. Then we set off to Rusty's home, which took us about ten minutes. His home was closer to the school than mine. It seemed to take as long to climb the three flights of stairs up to his apartment as it did to walk there from school. When we arrived, his grandmother was there to greet us.

"Greet" was maybe too strong a word. Rusty's grandmother, Mrs. Swerdlow, more or less grunted at us when we arrived. She certainly didn't smile.

Because I never knew my grandparents, I didn't know how they were supposed to react when they saw their grandchildren. Maybe her reaction was typical. When she finally spoke, it was to let us know dinner would be in about an hour or whenever Rusty's father came home. I sensed the family's timetable was set by Mr. Swerdlow.

Rusty's grandmother had a distinctive look. She didn't look like any women I knew. She didn't look like my mother, Aunt Edna, or any of my teachers. Unlike Rusty, she was short, although I suspect at one time she might have been taller. Now she stooped, which distorted her height. She was curved. The hump in her back made her look like a camel. She had almost as much facial hair as a camel, too. Fortunately, it was white like the hair on her head. If it had been dark, her facial hair would have frightened me. She wore a navy blue dress with a white collar.

Because of the hump, her dress came way up at the back. Unlike Miss Rafferty, though, her stockings appeared to go all the way up. Mrs. Swerdlow had no knots at her knees. Despite her hump and facial hair, something told me that, at one time, Mrs. Swerdlow may have been an attractive woman. Now, she looked as if life had beaten her down.

Whatever simmered on the stove and roasted in the oven smelled good, which told me Mrs. Swerdlow was a good cook. I looked forward to Rusty's birthday dinner, despite his grandmother's underwhelming reception. While we waited, Rusty took me into their front room.

It was a pleasant room. My mother and I didn't have such a room in our apartment. And it had things in it I had seen only in the Sears catalog: a sofa, two armchairs, and what Rusty called a coffee table, as well as many other things, including lamps. I couldn't imagine having a table just for coffee. None of their furniture and accessories would have fit in our apartment. It barely fit in theirs.

During my first look around the room, I had missed one other big piece of furniture. Against one wall was an upright piano. It was made of dark wood and had designs carved on the front panel above the keys as well as down the front legs. The keys were a little yellow, which should have told me the piano was old. But, back then, I didn't have much experience with pianos, much less coffee tables, to know how either should look. Rusty must have seen my mouth and eyes were open wide. He asked, "Do you pay the piano?"

It took me a minute to snap back into his reality and comprehend what was before me. "No," I said. "Do you?"

"I'm learning how to play. I take lessons from my grandmother," Rusty said.

Just then, we heard the door to the apartment open and close. I guessed Rusty's dad was home. I could hear the noise water makes when it splashes against the sink. I guessed he was washing his hands. When I heard someone with a low voice ask about dinner, I was certain it was Rusty's dad. I expected him to come into the front room to say hello to his son and his son's friend Marcus.

I didn't have to wait long. A tall man came in to the living room. He had dark hair, not white like Mrs. Swerdlow's or ginger like Rusty's. He said nothing to Rusty but turned to me and asked, "What's your name, kid?"

"Marcus," I said.

"What kind of name is that?" he asked. I explained to him that I was named after a Roman emperor and my father came from Catania.

Even I was surprised by my forthrightness. I guess Mr. Swerdlow was surprised, too, because all he said was, "Oh."

Mr. Swerdlow walked across the room to the piano. I thought he might sit and play. Not so. Instead, he reached up toward a glass pitcher on top of the piano, took out the stopper, and poured some amber liquid into a small glass that was next to the pitcher. Then he turned, walked back, and sat in one of the two armchairs where he sipped from the small glass. He said nothing, and neither did we. A few minutes later, he walked across the room toward the piano again. He reached up for the pitcher, took out the stopper, and poured more of the amber liquid into his glass. As before, he turned, walked back, and sat in the armchair where he continued to sip from his glass.

Mr. Swerdlow said nothing, and neither did we. I sensed this was a nightly ritual for Rusty's father. I also figured out why Rusty spoke so little. No one in his household seemed to talk about anything. Mr. Swerdlow repeated his trip to the piano at least two more times. I took my cue from Rusty. He said nothing, so I said nothing. We sat in silence. Finally, we heard Rusty's grandmother's voice. It broke the silence like the sudden start of a jackhammer on concrete. She called us for dinner.

My nose had not betrayed me. The meal Mrs. Swerdlow served was everything I hoped it would be. First, she served us a thick vegetable soup with a tomato-based broth. I watched Rusty. He waited for his father to pick up his spoon. Rusty followed his father's lead, and I took mine from Rusty. After a few seconds, his father took a big chunk of bread from a basket on the table and smothered it with butter. Rusty followed his father's lead, and I took mine from Rusty. Both the soup and bread were delicious. Then Mrs. Swerdlow served us roast beef, mashed potatoes, green beans, and gravy. Although the roast beef was cut paper thin, the portion was generous.

And, like the soup, this part of the meal was equally delicious. The Swerdlows may not have placed much value on conversation, but they sure placed a lot of value on a good and hearty meal.

The way they ate their meals was as routine as the way Rusty's father sipped his amber liquid. I didn't believe they acted this way for my benefit because nothing about it made me feel welcome. Instead, I felt like an interloper. I hoped the birthday celebration part of the evening would start soon. Surely things would liven up for Rusty's sake, if not mine.

As Mrs. Swerdlow collected our empty dinner plates from the table, she suggested we go into the front room where she would serve coffee and cake. Now I hoped to see the coffee table in action.

Mr. Swerdlow, Rusty, and I went into the living room. Mr. Swerdlow took the same armchair as before. Rusty and I sat at opposite ends of the sofa. After a minute or two, Rusty's father rose up from his chair and walked across the room toward the piano. As he had before dinner, he reached up for the pitcher, took out the stopper, and poured more amber liquid into his glass. As before, he turned, walked back, and sat in the armchair where he sipped from his glass.

Rusty's grandmother walked into the living room. She carried two cups and saucers, which I assumed, based on her earlier comments, contained coffee. She sat them down on the table. I had never tasted coffee. The bad news was I wasn't about to now, either. It turned out one cup was for Mr. Swerdlow and the other was for Rusty's grandmother. But the good news was, I now knew all about coffee tables. They're for coffee. After Rusty's grandmother finished her coffee, she announced it was time for cake. She got up from her armchair and left the room. Hallelujah, I thought. Rusty's birthday party is about to start.

Mrs. Swerdlow returned to the front room. She carried a tray, which she placed on the coffee table. Apparently, this table was for more than just coffee. On the tray were plates, forks, and a cake. The cake was covered in white icing. I didn't see any candles, but there was cake, and I hoped it was a chocolate.

"I think we should all sing 'Happy Birthday' to Rusty," said Mrs. Swerdlow as she walked toward the piano. Imagine my surprise when she didn't reach for the glass pitcher. Instead, she sat, put her hands on the keys, and started to play "Happy Birthday." I was so surprised that it took me a few seconds to find my voice. By the next "Happy birthday to you," I chimed in. Rusty beamed. For the first time, he smiled. He even sang along.

After we finished singing "Happy Birthday," Mrs. Swerdlow returned to her armchair and cut the cake. Because I was a guest, Mrs. Swerdlow said I should receive the first piece. Because it was Rusty's birthday, I wanted him to have it. So I passed it along to him.

Once the cake was cut, I could see it was chocolate. Mr. Swerdlow scowled as he sipped. The next piece of cake went to him. He put his down on the table. Rusty's grandmother handed me the third piece of cake. I was just about to pick up my fork and take a big bite when, out of the corner of my eye, I saw Rusty put his plate down on the table, too. What else could I do? I put my plate down on the table. Mrs.

Swerdlow picked up the tray and returned to the kitchen. I had no idea when we were going to eat our cake.

After a few moments of complete silence, Mr. Swerdlow mumbled. I wasn't sure, but I think he said that he wanted Rusty to play something on the piano for Marcus. It was a guess on my part. His words came out of his mouth the same way they came out of my mother's mouth after she drank several beers or when one of her mysterious voices took hold. As a result, I worried about what would happen next.

When I saw Rusty walk across the room toward the piano, sit on the seat, and put his hands on the keys, I knew I had heard Mr. Swerdlow correctly. "Play 'Moonlight Sonata,'" snapped Mr. Swerdlow. For some reason, Rusty stood. Then I saw him start to lift the lid on the piano bench. Before Rusty had raised the lid more than three inches, his father snapped again. "What are you doing? I told you to play."

"I was getting the music book," said Rusty.

"You don't need any book. You should know that piece by now. Just play!" Mr. Swerdlow's voice was so loud, the cups and saucers rattled on the coffee table.

Rusty sat down and put his hands on the piano keys. This time, his hands shook, but he started to play. As someone who had never heard "Moonlight Sonata," I couldn't tell how well or how poorly Rusty played. It sounded good to me. I was impressed that Rusty could play the piano, without the benefit of his music book and under the duress of his father's commands.

Apparently, Rusty didn't play well enough for his father. Mr. Swerdlow barked, "That was terrible. You're useless. Try another piece. Play 'English Country Garden.'" Rusty's hands shook even more. He started to play. It sounded good to me. However, before Rusty had completed more than several bars, Mr. Swerdlow yelled, "Stop, start again, and play it right this time." I saw Rusty's shoulders slump. He took a deep breath. His hands never left the keys. They still shook. He started to play. It sounded good to me. I was focused on Rusty and I was awed by his talent. I saw a side of him I had never seen at school.

As I watched Rusty play the piano, I didn't watch his father. Otherwise, I would have seen him stand, pull his belt out of his pant loops, fold it, head across the room, and strap Rusty across his back. I saw the first whack, which startled me. I saw the second whack, which scared me. I saw the third whack, which petrified me. By now I was afraid that Mr. Swerdlow would strike me, too.

Despite my fears, I gathered my wits. I stood up, ran out of the living room into the kitchen, past Mrs. Swerdlow, out the door, down the stairs, out to the street, and headed home. I ran and ran and ran and ran as fast as I could. I didn't look down. I didn't look up. I stared straight ahead. I completed a journey that usually took forty-five minutes in thirty minutes.

Never before, nor since, have I ever been so frightened. I couldn't begin to imagine what Rusty endured. I didn't want to know. The whole incident was beyond anything I had ever experienced. My mother may have been different, quirky even, but she never hit me. That night, I had an epiphany. I gave up my lifelong dream for a father.

Chapter 8
Spotted

When I felt lonely or if I wanted to ignore the world around me,
I focused on my sidewalk spots. During school hours, I paid no
attention to them. They were out of sight, so they were out of mind.
The playground had lots of spots, but they weren't sidewalk spots.
On my walks home from school, however, I could clear my brain of
classroom clutter. I stared at my sidewalk spots. They were my refuge.
I could actually tune out the world and reflect on nothing except
my sidewalk spots. They gave me great solace and incredible joy.
Sometimes, I focused too much on them and I found myself bumping
into other people. Because I was small, I was ignored.

One day, however, I heard a young girl shriek: "What do you think
you are you doing?" The shrillness of her voice and sharpness of her
command interrupted my contemplative bliss. I looked up. I moved
my head from right to left to find out who yelled and at whom. In the
doorway between two buildings, I saw Mary Ellen Henderson.

"Were you speaking to me?" I asked.

"Who else?" she replied with equal shrillness and sharpness. With
her hands firmly planted on her hips, Mary Ellen Henderson went
on to say, "Marcus, if you don't look up, you are going to walk into
someone or something."

I didn't know how to respond. First, I was surprised to find out
Mary Ellen knew my real name. By now, all my classmates called me
Playdough. Mary Ellen was smart and everything I wasn't. We had
never exchanged a single word in class. Yet, here she was calling me
Marcus. Secondly, I was surprised she cared if something happened

to me, good or bad. Thirdly, I didn't know what to tell her. My spots were my spots. I had never shared them with anyone.

I came up with a fib. I told Mary Ellen I liked to look for coins on the way home. "Coins!" she exclaimed. "What for?"

I told another fib. I said, "I want to buy some marbles so I can play with the other guys at school."

"Why do you hang around with those guys?" Although I admired Mary Ellen, I didn't like her derisiveness. "And why would you want to gamble? It's a sin."

I told her that Nobby and Rusty were my friends. I liked them and they liked me. As to her comments about marbles and sin, she took me by surprise. I didn't know what to say. I couldn't think of another fib.

Mary Ellen sighed, took a deep breath, and said, "I see. I'm happy you have friends." Then she said something that astounded me. Mary Ellen asked if we could be friends.

"Sure!" I said. "Why not?"

Mary Ellen smiled and said, "Great, see ya tomorrow, Marcus."

I continued to walk home. My mind swirled with all kinds of questions. I didn't even bother to look at my sidewalk spots. Why would someone as smart as Mary Ellen want to be friends with the likes of me? What would Nobby and Rusty say when I told them tomorrow? Or should I even tell them? Would Mary Ellen want to be friends with them, too? If I played marbles, did it make me a gambler and a sinner? Was it a sin to gamble? I knew Mary Ellen was smart, but something told me I should consult with a higher authority. I was Catholic enough to know marbles might be sin, but not Catholic enough to know for sure. But, who could I talk to for answers to all my questions?

Mary Ellen was smarter than Nobby and Rusty. So I knew neither of them could answer my questions. I knew my mother wouldn't know or want to know. Maybe Aunt Edna would know, but something told me her religion might make marbles a sin and off limits. Maybe she would have a new "uncle" who could give me advice. Meanwhile, I took solace in the notion I now had another friend. A few weeks ago, all I had were my spots, and now I had four new friends. The whole time I was looking down, things were looking up.

That night, when my mother asked me about school, I said, "It was fine." I said nothing to her about my discussion with Mary Ellen, marbles, sin, or anything else. This became a pattern.

The older I got, the less I said to my mother. My friends were my confidants. Still, the next day, I said nothing to Nobby or Rusty about my encounter with Mary Ellen. It wasn't a secret. I just didn't know how to explain it to them. No, I decided it was better to wait and see. When I found someone who could offer good advice and what I wanted to hear, I would then, and only then, ask my questions. It didn't take long.

Chapter 9
Aside

When I woke up on Saturday, I was confident I would get answers to all my questions. As always, I expected Aunt Edna would be along shortly. With luck, she would bring a boyfriend, and I would be able to ask him if it's a sin to play marbles and gamble. However, this Saturday, she came alone. As a result, I was left to ponder my many questions. I was concerned there would be no answers and no relief in sight.

Sunday, while I was sitting in church, the answer came to me. Why hadn't I thought of it before? It was so obvious. After Mass was over, I would ask Father O'Riley if it's a sin to play marbles. He would know. That's his job! He was the expert on sins. Of course, if I wanted to speak with him alone, I would have to wait until after all the other parishioners shook his hand and left the church.

I knew it could take a long while, which meant I would also have to come up with a good explanation as to why it took me so long to get home after Mass. My mother didn't like me to dawdle. Marbles had started to take over my life before I even owned my first marble or rolled my first shooter, but I had to know if was a sin to play. So I waited and waited until the last parishioner shook Father O'Riley's hand.

Finally, it was my turn. I stepped forward and put out my hand. Father O'Riley looked down at me. His expression was quizzical. Did he recognize me or didn't he? I wasn't sure. He extended his hand and said, "Good morning. Aren't you the little Hanlon boy? Marcus, isn't it?" So he knew me after all.

"Yes, Father," I said.

"I suppose you want to ask me about your First Communion?"

Of course, the thought of my First Communion had not even crossed my mind, but I wasn't going to let him know. I said, "Yes, Father, and I have another question to ask you, too."

Father O'Riley told me to have my mother contact the parish office and make arrangements for my First Communion classes. I said I would. Then, I took the big plunge. It took all my courage. Who knows where courage comes from? But when something is important to you and consumes all your thoughts, you dig deep and go for it. As Nobby always says, "A guy's gotta do what a guy's gotta do."

So I did it. I asked the big question: "Father O'Riley, is it a sin to play with marbles?"

Father O'Riley looked even more quizzical than he did before. Then he looked ponderous. Now I started to worry. Had I crossed a line? Had I committed a sin just because I asked the question? If so, what type of sin was it? Was I going to hell before I even left church? I couldn't tell by the look on his face. Father O'Riley rubbed his chin. What could it mean? Was this an even bigger sin than anyone in the whole Roman Catholic Church had ever committed before?

Father O'Riley put his hand down. He chuckled. I knew then I wasn't going to hell. He explained that the game of marbles, like bingo or card games, is not a sin unless it takes over your life. "If you become obsessed with marbles, if you become greedy, if you covet the marbles you win over the game itself, if you worship those activities more than all else, then it's sinful. Does that help explain the difference to you, Marcus?"

"Yes, Father," I replied. I am not sure if he noticed the sound of relief in my voice. The weight of the world and the threat of eternal damnation had been lifted from my shoulders. Father O'Riley bid me goodbye with an admonishment to have my mother call about First Communion.

I left church a happy boy. Not only did I have an answer to my question, but I also had an excuse to give my mother, and most importantly, I was a little smarter, at least about marbles, than Mary Ellen Henderson. I walked home in triumph. I didn't even bother to look at my sidewalk spots. I didn't need to.

Chapter 10
Walk On

Marbles never took over my life. Instead, marbles made way for other games such as softball, baseball, touch football, and all kinds of other sports that came and went. Most sports depended on the season or who had a ball. I was never very good at any sport. But the other kids didn't seem to mind, probably because they weren't very good at sports, either. I don't remember many sports stars at our school. The important thing was that I played with them and they played with me. Thanks to Mary Ellen Henderson, I even got to try to skip rope. As it turned out, I was pretty good, so much so that Mary Ellen invited me to skip double dutch. As I recall those days, I remember we enjoyed wholesome fun.

I wish I could say the same thing about Nobby and his kind of fun. His fun didn't seem as wholesome. Marbles never took over my life, but Nobby let marbles, cards, and other games of chance take over his life. He never missed an opportunity to gamble. If we played ball, he played just to bet. To this day, I'm not sure how well he did after his first game of marbles. My guess is if he had been successful, the other kids wouldn't have played with him. But the other kids did play with him, which meant they must have won, too.

Nobby didn't seem to let his losses get him down. If his number of wins didn't increase, his vocabulary did. Not only did he continue to call the other players chumps and pigeons, he called them stooges, suckers, marks, and a host of other names, none of which endeared him to me or anyone else. I started to wonder if Playdough was such a good nickname after all. Just the same, Nobby, Rusty, and I stayed friends. We just played different games, and we played them differently.

My mother called the church about my First Communion classes, just as Father O'Riley asked. For the second time in my life, I sensed her pride in me. It seemed my First Communion was as important to her as my first day of school. For the big day, she bought me a new outfit. I was surprised by what she chose because I would never wear it again. It was white, all white. She bought white shirt, white shorts, white socks, and even white shoes! When I tried the outfit on, even I thought I looked good, a little chunky maybe, but good. It was years later before I learned that if I wanted to look slim, I should wear black. I wondered if I had deceived myself about my appearance those many years ago. I may have deceived myself about another issue before I received my First Communion.

As part of my communion classes, I learned about the sacraments. I learned about reconciliation and penance and fasting. I learned many things about my religion. It was a lot to take in. It was serious stuff, and I took it seriously. I wanted to be ready when the big day came. I wanted to be worthy of the white suit, white shorts, white socks, and white shoes. In particular, I didn't want to let my mother down. She had invested a lot in my wardrobe, and by extension, in me. I also didn't want to let Father O'Riley down. Most importantly, I didn't want to let God down. The pressure was enormous. First Communion made me nervous. I took refuge in my sidewalk spots and bit my nails more than usual.

On the big day, my mother and Aunt Edna accompanied me to church. I joined the other First Communicants at the back of the church while my mother and Aunt Edna took their places as close to the front as they could find room. They sat about eight pews back from the altar on the right-hand side. As we stood in line, my knees knocked, my palms sweated, and my fingers were in my mouth. I chewed and chewed my nails as if my very life depended on them.

From the back, someone said, "Stand straight beside your partner; we will walk down the aisle in five minutes." Five minutes seemed to take forever. I wondered if I had enough fingernails left to get me through it. Then it hit me: I was five minutes from the biggest event in my life, and I had already broken an important rule. My whole relationship with my mother, with Father O'Riley, and with God was in jeopardy because I broke my fast to eat my fingernails before I received the sacrament of First Communion. Would go straight to hell? Now, not only was I paralyzed with First Communion fear, I was terrified over the thought that I would receive First Communion after I broke my fast with something as unseemly as fingernails. Why hadn't I stuck to my sidewalk spots rather than my fingernails to allay my fears? How could I have been so stupid? What was I going to do now? Who would I ask for advice? I had to think fast about fasting.

When I shake with fear, it's tough for me to think straight. But I managed to come up with a plausible excuse. I told myself that fingernails aren't food. I didn't eat them to satisfy my hunger. To be honest, I really didn't know why I ate them. They just seemed to show up in my mouth whenever I got bored or nervous. Suddenly, I calmed down. I no longer shook. That's it—I didn't break my fast because fingernails aren't food. That's what I told myself. I was going to be okay after all. I had escaped fingernail damnation. I was convinced, as any seven-year-old boy could be, that I was going to be okay with my mother, Father O'Riley, and most importantly, God.

The service began. Twelve of us, in pairs, marched down the aisle to the front of the church where we were met by Father O'Riley. My thoughts were scrambled, but my heart was full. My heart was full because of the solemnity and importance of my First Communion and because my mother was there. Her presence made it special. She showed me that she cared.

After communion, the congregation held a reception in the hall next to the church. After the reception, my mother suggested we go out for lunch and wondered aloud where we should go to eat. My mouth dropped, and Aunt Edna's mouth dropped. Neither of us knew what to say. We'd never heard my mother ever make such a suggestion, much less ask us for our opinion. Before we could close our mouths and answer, my mother said, "How about Sears for some pancakes?" Now I knew, for sure, this was a very special day. It was better than any birthday or even Christmas. Any thoughts about how I almost jeopardized this event evaporated. Memories of my First Communion and my sidewalk spots kept me going during the days when my mother couldn't have cared less where I wanted to go or what I wanted to eat.

Chapter 11
Walk Up

Like me, Nobby, Rusty, Mary Ellen Henderson, Chubby Hershberg, and even Piggy Jameson graduated from the eighth grade. We started high school together. We left Miss O'Hara, Mrs. Sturgess, and Miss Rafferty behind for a host of new high school teachers. The big difference between elementary school and high school was that we didn't have the same teachers all day. As a result, it was difficult to get to know any of them very well. We no sooner sat at our desk for one class when the bell rang and it was time to get up and change rooms to attend another class: biology, geography, history, mathematics, Spanish, physical education, or my favorite, shop.

It took me almost a month to figure out when and where I was supposed to be and equally long to make sure I had all the correct textbooks for the right class. There was nothing worse than to find all I had was a copy of *The Merchant of Venice* when I arrived at my mathematics class. Okay, maybe it was worse to show up for physical education without my gym shorts and shoes.

Our physical education teacher, Mr. Brandon, was tough and mean. Nobby said it was because he had been a drill sergeant in the war. I don't know how Nobby knew this, but it made sense. Mr. Brandon had no patience for students who forgot their gym shorts or their shoes. It meant a detention. His was no ordinary detention. Mr. Brandon's did not take place in the detention room where students were expected to complete math questions. His took place in the gymnasium where students were expected to report in the appropriate gym shorts and shoes.

Thankfully, I experienced a Mr. Brandon detention just once. As required, I reported to the gymnasium at the end of the school day. I stood in line with a couple of other students who were guilty of similar offenses. We waited for Mr. Brandon to appear. None of us knew what to expect because Mr. Brandon never meted out the same punishment from one detention to the next. His punishment depended on his mood. So far, no one had successfully been able to figure out his mood. To me, his mood was always bad. So I knew I was in for something tough and strenuous.

Mr. Brandon arrived and checked each name off his list. Then he ordered me and the others to run fifteen laps around the track. My first thought was that this detention won't be too bad until I remembered it was cold and rainy outside. Any further thoughts were interrupted by Mr. Brandon's booming voice: "Move it!" he yelled. We did. Each lap seemed to take forever. I never looked forward to a hot shower more. I never forgot my gym shorts and shoes again either.

Like me, Rusty received detentions from time to time and admitted to them. I can't say the same thing about Nobby. The rumor was that Nobby held not only the class record for detentions but the school record as well. Another rumor was that Nobby had more detentions than all his brothers combined. If a few detentions were a barometer of school performance, Rusty and I did well. We kept our noses clean throughout high school. Nobby was a different story. As much as he liked to brag about just about everything, Nobby never let on to us about his detentions. He was silent. I hoped he viewed detentions as losses rather than wins. Despite what we heard through the rumor mill, Nobby led Rusty and me to believe he spent his after-school hours doing what he liked best—he gambled. Of course, he claimed he won every game and every bet.

Before the first school bell of the day, Nobby, Rusty, and I met in front of the school and talked about the day ahead. After the last school bell of the day, we would meet once again in front of the school and review what happened during the day. As usual, Rusty never had much to say. Nobby always had a lot to say.

Unlike me, Rusty grew during the summer months between elementary and high school. He seemed about a foot taller. His voice dropped, and he seemed to speak an octave lower. Rusty also developed an athletic build marked by broad shoulders and a narrow waistline. Girls liked to be around him. Nobby also looked as if he had grown eight to ten inches taller. Yet he was every bit as skinny as he was in elementary school. His elbows and knees were every bit as boney. His face, however, became more angular. He called it chiseled. His voice was lower, too. Me, well, I was still short and plump, although I grew a couple of inches. I no longer had to roll up the bottom of my pants. My voice cracked when I spoke. Despite the changes in Nobby and me, we didn't attract the girls in the same way Rusty attracted them. But they didn't dislike being around us, either.

Despite our friendship and the amount of time we spent together throughout the remaining years of elementary school and throughout high school, Rusty and I never spoke about the incident at his birthday party. He knew that I knew his father was a mean man. Over the years, and thanks to my friendship with Rusty, I learned true friends can develop a relationship that doesn't require introspection, dissection, and discussion. These types of friendships are distinguished by a bond often characterized by unspoken and almost psychic communication. They are also the types of friendships that allow you to pick up where you left off, even if five, ten, or twenty years go by.

Rusty was this kind of friend to me. It didn't matter that he towered over me or that he was much more popular than I was.

It was no surprise to anyone when Rusty told us one morning that he had been picked to play on the junior football team. He looked like a football player, and now he would be one. And play he did.

In just a few games, Rusty showed his prowess on the gridiron. He could throw, he could catch, but most importantly, he could run. He scored touchdown after touchdown for our school team. In no time, Rusty became a star. During lunch hours, everyone wanted to sit with him—the other football players, the baseball players, the track athletes, and the girls—the really pretty ones.

When our lunch periods coincided, Rusty and I would sit together. No matter how popular Rusty became, he always had time for me. By virtue of my friendship with Rusty, I became more popular, too. If Rusty liked me, it was enough for other people to like me, too. Nobby never joined us for lunch. He was always busy. Nobby spent his lunch periods across the street from school and in front of the variety store where he played cards with anyone who would play for money or anything dear to him such as cigarettes, Coca-Cola, or potato chips.

On any given lunch period on any school day, at least a dozen guys would be in front of the variety store. All were students. Some went for a smoke. Some went to get away from school for a little while. Some went to play cards. Some, like Nobby, did all three and more. By the end of the ninth grade, Nobby was more involved in games of chance than he was in school.

Card games had pretty much become Nobby's way of life. He tolerated school, but Nobby lived to bet. Sometimes he bet on card games. Sometimes he bet on football teams. Sometimes he bet on baseball teams. Sometimes he bet on boxers. But all the time, you could count on Nobby to gamble. Rusty and I had no idea how well Nobby gambled. From time to time, he would be without his favorite San Francisco 49ers football jacket. When we asked him where it was, he was always non-committal. We suspected he had lost it as part of a bet. Within a few days, we would see him with his 49ers jacket again draped over his shoulders. During four years of high school, his jacket disappeared and reappeared at least one hundred times.

Chapter 12
Side Tracked

I have no idea why the owner of a variety store put up with the students who spent their time on the sidewalk in front of his place of business. They made it difficult for others to get into the store, especially when the students held a card game. But whatever money students spent went toward cigarettes or soda, which may have made it tolerable to the owner. The store was called Shorty's, and everyone called the man behind the counter Shorty. I don't know why. None of us were sure he was the actual owner. None of us were brave enough to ask him, either. He wasn't short. He wasn't tall. I would have called him Average.

The variety store was anything but average. In hindsight, it could best be described as below average, but students, and more importantly, neighbors relied on it for various and sundry items. Its distinctive smell hit us first when we walked through the front door. It wasn't a bad smell, but it wasn't one anyone would bottle and sell as a perfume next to Evening in Paris or Chanel No. 5. I never was able to detect the source or sources of the odor. I suspect it was a combination of scents. Part of the odor probably came from tobacco.

Shorty's carried all kinds of tobacco products. He sold cigars, chewing tobacco, pipe tobacco, pipes, pipe cleaners, cigarette tobacco, cigarette papers, and cigarettes. Within the cigarette line, Shorty's offered plain, filtered, menthol, regular, long, extra long, and extra-extra long. Unlike other stores that sold cigarettes in a sealed package, Shorty's would break the seal on a package and sell the cigarettes individually. Shorty didn't have age restrictions, either. If we could reach the counter, we could buy two cigarettes for twenty-five cents.

Lots of students bought them this way. Just before payday, lots of area residents bought them this way, too.

Cigarettes weren't the only thing that could be bought piecemeal at Shorty's. In the dairy case, eggs were available by the dozen, by the half-dozen, or by the egg. Similarly, Shorty's sold fruit and vegetables by the piece. By the entrance of the store, Shorty's had two large baskets. Each was lined with what was supposed to look like grass. Once upon a time, it may have looked like grass, but when I was a high school student, it looked like a chunk of carpet a funeral home might use to surround a burial site on a rainy day. One of the baskets held fruit. In it, a customer might find a several apples in various stages of ripeness, a few oranges, and early in the week, some bananas. The other basket held vegetables. In it, a customer might find several potatoes, a few onions, and some carrots. Besides a dairy cooler, there were two other coolers. One held beer and wine. The other held sodas. Shorty's carried every type of soda including Coca-Cola, Pepsi, 7Up, and Royal Crown Cola. Of course, he also offered what my Aunt Edna called mixers—tonic water, club soda, and ginger ale. Best of all, Shorty's carried my favorites, Orange Crush and Grape Crush.

The walls inside the store must have had a thousand long nails that stuck out. These nails held just about anything anyone could imagine. From sewing kits to socks and from dog collars to dust mops, no nail was left empty. It was easy to tell what sold well and what didn't by the amount of dust on top of each item.

Of course Shorty's store also had rows of shelves. From cleaning fluids to cat food, from paper towels to dog food, no shelf space was left empty. And, just like the stuff that hung on the walls, it was easy to tell what sold well and what didn't by the dust on top of each item. I don't believe Shorty ever dusted. I don't believe Shorty ever took inventory, either. It would be just plain too difficult to count every item in the store.

In front of the checkout counter there were racks of candy bars and bags of potato chips, corn chips, and cheese puffs. On top of the counter were four large glass jars. Each held a different type of loose candy. Some candies were wrapped and some were unwrapped. One jar could contain Tootsie Rolls, which were wrapped. Another jar could contain orange slices, which were unwrapped. A jar might contain something different each week, or as a few months could go by without a change in a candy jar. No one knew what sold or didn't sell except Shorty.

Although Shorty called some of those treats "penny candies," they cost more than a penny. The size, type, and wrap, if any, of each candy determined its cost. Each could cost as much as five cents. I never bought unwrapped candy. The thought of Shorty putting his knuckled and unwashed hand into the jar to pull out an unwrapped piece of candy had no appeal, even to a guy who lived in the Tenderloin.

I was never sure what was under the checkout counter at Shorty's. Although the countertop was glass, it had become scratched and etched over the years. Now, whatever was underneath could no longer be seen. If any item under the counter, on the wall, or on a shelf had a "sell by" date, it didn't matter. Supermarkets' rules didn't seem to apply to Shorty's. Any and all items lasted in the store until they sold. I was mesmerized by how much Shorty was packed into that store.

No one bothered to look down when they entered Shorty's or when they walked around. If they did, what would they find? They would find well-worn remnants of linoleum. It had long lost its pattern and was unattractive. Out of the linoleum popped traces of splintered floor boards. Is it any wonder, then, I was unable to find the source of the smell? It could have easily been from something that oozed up from the ground or tobacco remnants or spilled beer.

The door to Shorty's was always open. I never knew if it closed at night or if anyone other than Shorty stood behind the counter. Despite the product congestion, Shorty's was always tidy, inside and out, although not necessarily clean. I never saw any wrappers or cigarette butts on the sidewalk. Sometime during the day, Shorty must have used a broom, even if he never used a duster.

Shorty had something outside he didn't have inside. What he had excited me more than even Orange or Grape Crush. Shorty had the best sidewalk spots in all of San Francisco. In my opinion, they were worthy of an exhibit at the Smithsonian. They could have held my attention for hours at a time. I didn't spend hours with them because I would have interfered with the card players and the flow of customers. But I was comforted to know they were there and would always be there if and when I needed them. The great thing about sidewalk spots is there are always other places were I can find them. I've never felt the desperation other collectors must feel when a certain coin, postage stamp, or work of art is out of reach.

Shorty's had no real competition in the area. While other businesses occupied spaces on both sides of the store and all sides of the block, Shorty's was the only variety store. On one side of Shorty's was a bakery. It sold bread, pastries, and doughnuts. The bakery was called Panetteria. Every bakery purchase was placed in a white paper bag or in a white cardboard box. The shop was spotless. So was the sidewalk out front. The counters, the display cases, the shelves, and even the walls were white. The ladies who ran the store wore white dresses covered by white aprons. On their heads, they wore little white hats with nets to keep the hair off their necks. They even wore white stockings and white shoes. I had not seen so much white clothing since my First Communion. The baker spent most of his time in the back with the ovens, so we seldom saw him. But when we did see him, he was always dressed in white.

The bakery presented a contrast to Shorty's variety store. No one ever accused Shorty of selling fresh bread. No one ever accused Shorty of selling stale bread, either. Shorty's bread had an indefinite shelf life. As a result, the bakery didn't need to worry about any competition from Shorty, and he didn't need to stock much bread. What bread he did stock was white, already sliced, and packaged in plastic wrap marked by balls printed in red, yellow, and blue with the name Wonder printed in red. Wonder was an apt name. To this day, I wonder how it kept so long without going stale. Once, I managed to keep a loaf in the refrigerator for three months without any trace of mold. I couldn't say the same about Panetteria's rolls or doughnuts. I never knew how long they could last before going stale. They were so good, I finished them within minutes.

On the other side of Shorty's variety store, there was a small Italian restaurant. In addition to the tables inside, the restaurant had three tables outside with big umbrellas that, when opened, stood four feet above each table. The umbrella poles stuck through the centers of the tables down to large metal plates that looked like fancy sewer-hole covers to keep the umbrellas in place. The umbrellas were made of green and white panels with Martini & Rossi printed in black over a big red dot on the white panels. But the name of the restaurant wasn't Martini & Rossi—it was called Luigi's.

The only time I had heard anything called "martini" was at a dinner with Aunt Edna and one of my uncles. They ordered martinis. When the waiter brought their martinis to our table, I discovered they had ordered drinks in fancy glasses. At that time, we weren't in an Italian restaurant, so I wondered what Martini & Rossi had to do with an Italian restaurant like Luigi's.

Although I had an Italian first name, claimed to be from Catania, and was now in the ninth grade, I knew nothing about Italian food. The Italian dishes posted on the menu outside the restaurant were all in a foreign language to me. I couldn't pronounce the names of items posted on the menu, much less guess what went into such items as lasagna and ravioli. I'd say it was all Greek to me, except it was Italian. What were these things? Who would eat them? As far as I knew, they could be made of exotic plants, tropical fish, or wild beasts.

About halfway down the menu, I was happy to recognize one item, spaghetti. Sometimes, our high school cafeteria served that dish. Just when I thought I might be able to order from the menu without making a fool of myself, I noticed "Bolognese" was written next to spaghetti. What was Bolognese? This was not something our high school cafeteria served. All the dishes were as foreign to me as, well, Italy. They were not something my mother served. I doubted if she knew anything about them, either.

Luigi's Italian restaurant was a popular place. At lunch time, the tables inside and out were always full. Whenever I walked by, I was captivated by the aromas from the restaurant each time the front door opened and the waiter placed another dish before another diner. So how bad could it be? Based on what I saw on plates, everything looked good, although everything seemed to come with something that looked like lumpy red gravy. I knew my mother would never go for this kind of gravy. Hers was a source of pride. My mother's gravy was brown, and it was always smooth and free of lumps.

By the eleventh grade, Nobby, Rusty, and I decided it was time for us to brave Luigi's for lunch. Any place that busy during lunchtime must be pretty good. At no time had we seen anyone leave Luigi's in an ambulance, nor had we heard any scuttlebutt from anyone else at school to suggest it would make us ill. To the contrary, many seniors on the football team told Rusty the pizza was great. We decided to give it a try. Unfortunately, none of the seniors had told Rusty what kind of pizza we should order.

Rusty, Nobby, and I stood in the open doorway of Luigi's. Pretty soon, an attractive woman with long dark hair came up to us and asked, "How many?"

I could tell by the look on Nobby's face that he itched to say something smart-alecky like "Look around, moron, how many do you think?"

Thankfully, he said nothing. I said, "Three, please." My mother would have been proud to hear me use a magic word. We were shown to a table. Because I had peeked in the window a few times, I already knew the inside tables didn't have umbrellas. However, I didn't know that, unlike the outside tables, the inside tables had white table cloths, white cloth napkins, and more silverware than I had ever seen any one person use. I started to feel that maybe the three of us were out of our depth, and maybe the cost of what we were about to order was beyond reach.

The woman with the long dark hair handed us each a menu and asked if we wanted water. I didn't know about the other guys, but my throat was dry. I was scared. We all asked for water.

Within a few minutes, she returned to our table and presented each of us with a glass of water. The glasses also contained ice. I knew I should sip my water, but I gulped it instead. The woman smiled. "You were thirsty. I'll get you more water. The waiter will be right with you." I was horrified the woman had seen me drink so quickly, but more horrified that we were going to have to place our order in just a matter of minutes.

The woman walked away and we opened the menus. "There's more than two pages!" Nobby exclaimed. Rusty directed us to page four, where the different types and sizes of pizza were listed. We stared at the page and discovered Luigi's offered eight different types of pizzas in three different sizes: nine inches, twelve inches, and eighteen inches. With just minutes to make our decision, we didn't have time to speculate about mozzarella, pepperoni, basil, and anchovies. We knew nothing about them. But we did know about cheese and tomato sauce. We also knew we only had so much money. So we were ready to order by the time the waiter arrived at our table.

My panic started to subside. We ordered a twelve-inch cheese and tomato sauce pizza. "Will there be anything else?" asked the waiter.

In unison, we answered, "No, that's all. Thank you, sir." What else could there be? We would have needed an Italian-English dictionary to figure out each item on the menu. We sat back in our chairs, let out collective sighs, and sipped our waters.

"For all the stuff on the table and what this joint is charging, I sure hope it tastes good," said Nobby, "otherwise, you won't see me in here again." I wished I had Nobby's bravado. Instead, I was still cowed by the ice cubes in the water glasses and all the silverware.

After our water glasses had been refilled two more times, the waiter placed a square stand in the center of our table and three white plates to the left of Rusty. A few minutes later, he returned. This time, he carried a large circular metal tray with our pizza. The waiter placed it on the stand. The pizza looked like it had already been cut into nine pieces. Although I could see tomato sauce peek through, the top of the pizza was white. What was that? Any cheese I had ever seen was always orange. I wondered about this white cheese, but I said nothing.

The waiter picked up what looked like a trowel from underneath the pizza, picked up one piece, put it on a plate, and placed it before Nobby. He repeated the process for Rusty and me. When he finished, the waiter said something like "Man gee, benny." We just shrugged our shoulders.

By now, we were beyond hungry. No amount of water had killed our appetites. We stared at our pieces of pizza. I could tell none of us knew what to do next. Nobby broke the silence. "How are we supposed to eat this, anyway?"

"Look around," said Rusty. "Most people are picking it up with their hands."

I remarked a few diners used knives and forks. "Then, I guess you do whatever you want." I was afraid I might drop my piece if I used my hands. So I picked up my knife and fork.

Rusty and Nobby picked their pieces up with their hands. Right away, the end of their pieces flopped down and they had to duck their heads to get underneath the ends. They succeeded and took their first bites. I tried to cut my piece while I watched them chew. "How is it?" I asked.

Both nodded their heads. "Like nothing I have ever tasted before, but good," said Rusty.

"Same here," said Nobby.

I took my first bite. I was a little apprehensive about the white stuff on top. I hoped it was just really pale orange cheese and nothing weird. As I chewed my first bite, I marveled. This was the moment I fell in love with Italian food. That was the moment I knew my blood was every bit as Italian as it was Irish. I later grew to love lasagna more than corned beef and cabbage. And I grew to love lumpy red sauce more than smooth brown gravy. I knew it would take a while to discover every item on Luigi's menu, but after my first bite of pizza, I knew it would be worthwhile.

Of all the stores in the area around our high school, Shorty's was the one we frequented most. Panetteria and Luigi's were stores we frequented when we had a little extra cash and could afford something special. Of course, the neighborhood had other restaurants, bars, and businesses including jewelry, women's clothing, shoe, and cutlery stores as well as a barbershop, a hair salon, and a bank. Because they were beyond my neighborhood, and I seldom had money anyway, I knew little about any of them except they all seemed to flourish and all had sidewalk spots. While they may have been blocks away from the Tenderloin, it didn't make them exempt from crime. Many times I would be on my way to school and see a door or window boarded up due to a recent breakin.

I never saw a boarded door or window at Shorty's. Maybe it was because Shorty's door was always open. If Shorty's had been the victim of crime, we would have heard about it from either Nobby or from any one of the many students who were in and out on any school day. Our city may have been large, but our school neighborhood was still small. Gossip and news traveled fast.

Chapter 13
Side by Side

I did okay in high school. I was neither an honor student nor a failure. I managed B's in most classes except English, Spanish, and physical education. In those three classes, I could barely manage a gentleman's C. I had no ear for languages, even my own. My size and my girth made any physical activity a challenge, though I tried. By the twelfth grade, I started to worry I might not graduate despite assurances from Nobby. "You're a shoo-in to get your diploma. Me, on the other hand, well, I may have to figure out another way to graduate." Nobby never shared what other way he had in mind. Frankly, I didn't want to know, because I suspected his way wasn't a legitimate one.

Even though it was eight months away, I worried about graduation. My worries were not so much for myself but for my mother and Aunt Edna. Neither had graduated from high school. They constantly lamented their failures to complete high school. They saw a graduation diploma as a ticket to a better job and a better life. So my graduation became more important to them than it did to me. They harped on its importance. Maybe they were the reason I worried so much.

At no time did my mother or Aunt Edna ever speak about anything other than the importance of a high school diploma. They never mentioned college. Maybe they didn't think I had the potential. Or maybe the idea of college was too foreign for them to even contemplate. I don't know. They never discussed college, although they often told me I could be anything I wanted to be. The problem was that I just wanted to be to be done with the twelfth grade and get my diploma. I would plan for the future the day after graduation—at least that's what I told Mary Ellen Henderson when she asked me about my plans.

We were in the library for study hall when Mary Ellen whispered, "I'm so excited about next year."

"Why?" I whispered back.

"Because I will go away to college."

I was nonplussed. Until then, it had never occurred to me that Mary Ellen, or any of us who had been together since elementary school, would go off in different directions. For some reason, which seemed silly when I thought about it later, I had always thought we would be together forever.

I guessed she could tell by the look on my face that I was startled by her college revelation. "Don't you have plans to go to college, too?" By now, a minute or two had elapsed. The magnitude of what Mary Ellen said had sunk in.

In eight months, we would go our separate ways. The thought of our future separation caused a little lump to form in the back of my throat. Now, on top of my worries about graduation, I had new worries about what I would do when I was all alone. What would I do without Mary Ellen, Rusty, and Nobby? Here I was seventeen years old, and I had to fight the urge to cry. In a split second, I realized how much I had staked my life on these three people who were probably going to desert me. I gathered my thoughts and let Mary Ellen know that all I wanted to do right now was simply pass the twelfth grade and receive my diploma.

"You'll graduate, Playdough. Why are you so worried?" I explained my difficulties with English and Spanish. I saw no need to mention physical education. Although she taught me how to skip rope, Mary Ellen knew as well as anyone I wasn't athletic. "Oh, Playdough, I can help you with English and Spanish. You should have asked me. Those are two of my best subjects."

All subjects were Mary Ellen's best subjects. Everyone knew it. She was an honor student. She always got straight A's. I'm not sure how she did in physical education. Apart form double dutch, I had never seen her play sports. I didn't care. Mary Ellen offered to help me, and I accepted her offer without hesitation. "I'll coach you after school on Mondays and Wednesdays. We can't meet on Tuesdays or Thursdays because I have piano and voice lessons on those days. We can meet right here in study hall. Let's start tomorrow. You identify the areas in which you need help." As always, Mary Ellen was confident. As always, I wasn't. Just the same, I left study hall less worried than I had been for weeks.

On the way home, I studied my sidewalk spots. I counted on them to guide me not only to my home but also during my time with Mary Ellen. I had to be ready for tomorrow's session with her. She would expect me to be prepared, and I didn't want to let her down. I wanted to make the months we had left count. More importantly, I wanted to graduate. I couldn't let my mother and Aunt Edna down. At the same time, I started to wonder about college. Mary Ellen took it for granted that I would go to college, too. What did she see in me I didn't see in myself? I stared and stared at my sidewalk spots for insight. They gave me no clue. Maybe I could work up the courage to ask Mary Ellen.

I took inventory of my English and Spanish issues. Vocabulary shouldn't have been a problem. After all, words in any language are just a bunch of scrambled consonants until the vowels are dropped in to make them understandable. The tricky part of English, for me, was how to link my sentences together to make paragraphs. If it was up to me, each sentence would form a different paragraph. When it came to Spanish, I was a long way from paragraphs. First, I had to get my head around words before sentence structure or paragraphs. I hoped Mary Ellen could show me the way in both languages.

We met in study hall the next day. Mary Ellen decided that, on Wednesdays, we would focus on English. On Mondays, we would focus on Spanish. Today was Wednesday, so we started with English. "In which areas do you have difficulty, Marcus?" Yesterday she called me Playdough when we spoke as friends. Today, she called me Marcus. I recognized the change in our relationship and wondered if Mary Ellen would revert to our usual familiarity once she was no longer my tutor.

I explained that my biggest problem was paragraphs. When I had to write a composition or book report, I didn't know what made up a paragraph. I didn't know when to finish one paragraph or when to start the next one. It didn't matter how many sentences I wrote, they wound up as one big paragraph. As a result, my English grade suffered. "Why, Marcus, I'm surprised you got this far in school and have this problem. It's an easy problem to solve. Let's take a look at your compositions, essays, and any other work you have submitted."

I didn't have all my previous English submissions with me, but I had a few, which were enough for us to make a start. I handed them to Mary Ellen. She picked up the first composition. It was on a single sheet of paper. She read it, which seemed to take her forever. Her face gave nothing away. I had no idea what she thought. Although she claimed mine would be an easy problem for us to solve, I was not as confident. I was afraid this session might test our friendship. I was afraid she would never call me Playdough again. Finally, Mary Ellen put the composition down. She put her head up. Her expression remained fixed. Then she said, "Marcus, I see we have our work cut out for us. Let's get down to basics."

Mary Ellen went on to explain what makes up a paragraph. I already knew on a philosophical basis. My problem was I didn't know what made up a paragraph on a practical basis. She must have sensed my exasperation. In response, Mary Ellen said something no English teacher had said to me before: "Marcus, you're good in geography.

Treat your composition as you would a geography report. Break it down into sections, where each section forms something different like a different country, a different state, or a different city. Pick up your pencil. Now that I have explained paragraph principles and given you a corollary, I want you to mark on the page where you think the first paragraph of your report ends."

I picked up my pencil. By "corollary," I assumed she meant an example, but I wasn't about to ask. First, because I didn't think I could say "corollary"; and second, because I didn't know for sure what it meant. So I reread my composition and kept in mind what she had told me. I looked for the first section in my composition and thought about different countries. What might distinguish one from another? To the extent I could look at my English composition as I would look at a geography report was a challenge. Then I made my first mark with my pencil.

"Now, look for the second, third, and any other sections and make more marks," Mary Ellen instructed. I took my time and continued to be mindful of her reference to geography. At first, it seemed to distract me. But as I took my time and did as she said, I began to make a connection. I could see that paragraphs defined groups of sentences about one idea in the same way that borders defined regions within a country. I hoped my interpretation was accurate. After I made all my pencil marks, I passed my paper back to Mary Ellen.

Mary Ellen picked up my paper and read it. Once again, it seemed to take her forever. Her face gave nothing away this time, either. I had no idea what she thought. I had no idea how I had done. All of a sudden, Mary Ellen said, "Playdough, you did it. You got it just as I knew you would!"

I couldn't begin to describe my euphoria. In a single session with Mary Ellen, I mastered the concept of paragraphs, which had eluded me since elementary school. More importantly, Mary Ellen called me Playdough instead of Marcus. I knew our friendship was intact. I thanked her profusely. She accepted my gratitude but reminded me our work had just begun. Mary Ellen gave me homework. She expected me to mark the paragraphs in all my previous English assignments. She promised me we would review them during next Wednesday's English tutorial session. Mary Ellen was insistent. She promised I would fully understand how to form paragraphs by the time she was through with me.

The thought of additional homework, thanks to Mary Ellen, did nothing to dampen my spirits as I made my way home. I didn't walk; I strode. I didn't look down. I didn't bother with my sidewalk spots as I held my head high. A good coach could make a difference in anyone's game. In my case, the game was paragraphs in English composition. I hoped Mary Ellen would have the same effect on me when we met on Monday for our Spanish tutorial. For now, though, I just let the joy of today's accomplishment cascade over me.

Over the weekend, I did as Mary Ellen asked. To prepare for next Wednesday's tutorial, I reviewed my previous English compositions and marked the paragraphs in each one. Meanwhile, I started to fret about Monday's Spanish session. Would Mary Ellen be able to come up with an equally simple solution to my problems with Spanish? I hoped so.

Monday after school, Mary Ellen and I met in the study hall as planned. I told her that over the weekend I had marked the paragraphs on my English compositions. "That's nice, Marcus, but we're here today for Spanish." It was back to Marcus again. Because she called me Marcus rather than Playdough, Mary Ellen let me know she meant business. This was not a time for friendship, even though these tutorial sessions were born out of our friendship. "Do you have any results from recent Spanish quizzes?" From my three-ring binder, I pulled out the results of four quizzes and handed them to her. She looked them over. As always, her facial expression gave no clue. After she finished her review of the third quiz results, she turned to me. "You do need help in Spanish." Unlike our English session, I sensed that she could offer no easy fix.

Mary Ellen passed the Spanish quizzes back to me. She was silent for many minutes. Those minutes seemed like hours. The quiet and stillness led me to believe she had no solutions and my situation was hopeless. I despaired. All of a sudden, she smiled. Then she said something that sounded like it was right out of *My Fair Lady*: "I think I've got it!" I hoped it wasn't another corollary. I still couldn't say "corollary," and I still didn't know what it meant. My hopes were dashed. "I have another corollary. Marcus, you're good in mathematics. So, we'll treat Spanish just like mathematical problems."

I couldn't wait to hear how Mary Ellen was going to draw these two vastly different subjects together so I could learn Spanish. "Marcus, do you remember how you learned times tables in the second and third grades?" I didn't recall. Mary Ellen reminded me the teacher used flash cards. "We're going to use them to help you learn Spanish. We'll create Spanish vocabulary and grammar flash cards based on each chapter of our Spanish textbook. As you create each flash card, you'll start to gain more familiarity with Spanish. If you use the flash cards for thirty minutes every day, you'll start to be more comfortable with the language." Her solution sounded plausible. I had hoped for one that required less time and effort, but I recognized hers was the best way to improve my grade.

"Open your textbook at chapter one." I did as I was told. "Now, pull out three blank pages from your binder. Fold each sheet into eighths and tear away at each fold so we wind up with twenty-four small but equally sized pieces of paper." I did as I was told. "On one side of each piece of paper, write a Spanish word in large print, and below the Spanish word, write the English translation in smaller print. On the reverse side of the piece of paper, write an English word in large print and below it write the Spanish translation in smaller print." I did as I was told. It took me a few minutes to get the hang of it. I passed each piece to Mary Ellen so she could review my work as I went along. She approved. I completed forty-eight cards in about forty-five minutes. By then, it was time for us to adjourn that day's study session. While I started to pack up, Mary Ellen instructed me to practice with the first set of flash cards at least thirty minutes per day. She also instructed me to make the same kinds of flash cards for chapters two though six and come prepared to show them to her the following Monday.

When I left our tutorial session, I didn't have the same bounce in my step as I did the previous Wednesday. I did have more confidence, though, and I didn't need to take refuge in my sidewalk spots. While I walked, my thoughts were devoted to the assignment I had to complete between now and next Monday. As before, Mary Ellen had come up with another great solution to another problem. It was a solution I could understand. More importantly, it was one I could manage. I now hoped that, beyond these Spanish and English translations on my flash cards, I would be able to translate these study sessions into better grades in both subjects.

Mary Ellen and I met twice a week for the rest of October, all of November, and the first week of December. During the second week of December, we sat for examinations. These exams would not only test our curriculum knowledge, but two of my examinations would also test the results of my English and Spanish study sessions with Mary Ellen. Since we started our tutorials, I had submitted two English compositions. My teacher offered no comments about paragraphs, so I assumed I had overcome this problem. My composition grades were better. Based on three Spanish pop quizzes, my grasp of Spanish showed improvement, too.

December 20, the last day of school before our Christmas and New Year's break, our homeroom teacher distributed our report cards. I wanted to wait and open mine later, but the other students in homeroom were checking theirs, so I checked mine. I was delighted

90

by what I saw. My grade in English had gone from a C minus to a B. And my grade in Spanish had gone from a D to a C plus. Overall, my average was a B. The only subject that pulled my average down was physical education. Mary Ellen could not help me overcome the challenges of gymnastics, basketball, and volleyball. For now, I would set aside those concerns and focus on what I had achieved, thanks to Mary Ellen. I could hardly wait to share the good news with her during our lunch break.

As I left school, I was gratified, and it was reflected in my walk. Rather than look down, I looked left and right. I took note of all the store windows, filled with Christmas decorations. I decided to linger in Union Square. Nowhere, at least as far as I know, are store windows more beautiful than in San Francisco. As I looked in each window, I wished I could afford to buy my mother and Aunt Edna one of the many nice things on display at Saks or Tiffany's. Alas, those things were beyond my means.

I wished I could buy something for Mary Ellen as a way to express my appreciation for everything she had done for me over the past couple of months. I had sent her a Christmas card, for which she expressed great thanks. However, it seemed to fall short. Perhaps I could make up for it later. Meanwhile, I savored San Francisco's sights and sounds of the season. Christmas was just five days away.

Chapter 14
Side Swiped

Christmas was different for me as a teenager than it was for me as a child. While the day's events were the same, the anticipation and hopes I associated with Christmas started to evaporate from the time I turned seven until now. Nonetheless, I still enjoyed Christmas because I could spend most of the day with my mother and Aunt Edna. We had a tradition.

Every Christmas Day, for as long as I can remember, my mother came home from the bar before her usual time. I'm not sure what time she got home because I was asleep. It was the one workday of the year when she was home to greet me when I awoke. She couldn't have slept for long, if at all. When I was younger, I thought she was on hand to make sure Santa Claus found the milk and cookies I put out for him before I went to bed. Every Christmas morning, the glass and plate were empty. So I knew Santa Claus had paid a visit.

Like all children, I started a long list of gifts I wanted Santa to bring. My mother did not discourage me. Every year, I made my list for Santa Claus. My mother mailed my list for me. She reminded me, though, that Santa Claus had millions of children just like me for whom he had to find presents. She also reminded me that he had one sleigh in which to put everything, and his reindeer were tiny. They had to pull a big and fully loaded sleigh. In her way, she appealed to my common sense and encouraged me to believe it was unfair for any child to expect Santa Claus to bring everything to everybody. Instead, she suggested that I set my sights on just one gift.

Somehow, between the time I completed my list and Christmas Day, she adjusted my expectations. No matter what I found under the tree on Christmas Day, I was always the happiest guy on earth. I never felt short changed. I realize now what she did over the years. It was no small feat to make a little boy want less rather than more. My mother wasted her talents cleaning bars. She should have sold used cars, run for political office, or both.

This year, like all the others, I saw one wrapped box under our Christmas tree. Ours was a small artificial tree, which I still have. Our tree had colored lights that shone intermittently and looked like they twinkled. On the top branch was a big gold star, which I also still have. Our tree also had ornaments on each branch along with tinsel that was supposed to look like icicles. I no longer have any of those. The tag on the wrapped box was made out to me with "Love from Santa." Even though I had learned the truth about Santa Claus many years before, my mother kept him alive. As I started to unwrap my gift, I wished I had played along and left out milk and cookies.

This year, like all the others, I received exactly what I wanted: a lumber jacket. Most of the kids at school had red plaid ones. Mine was blue plaid. Most often, I wanted to wear what all the other kids wore, but not this time. While I wanted the same style jacket, I wanted a different color. I'm not sure I ever conveyed my color preference to anyone. I was too old to write a letter to Santa. Yet, this year like all the others, Santa came through. I was a happy big boy who didn't want more. Because I was happy, I could tell my mother was happy, too. It felt good.

This year, like all the others, while my mother drank her coffee, I got ready for Mass. I wore my new plaid jacket and my brown hard-soled shoes.

Attendance at weekly Mass was always important in my life. Over time, I discovered attendance at holiday Mass was more important to others like my mother. On Christmas Day and other holidays, they crowded the church so regulars, like me, found it difficult to find a seat. I could always tell which parishioners came just for the holidays—they had swiveling heads. They sat and immediately looked around to see if the church had changed since their last visit. Of course, it hadn't changed. They should have known. If they hadn't made a contribution since their last visit, why did they think the church had undergone a transformation? Then I caught myself. How could I be so judgmental? After all, maybe they were the true believers. Maybe I was the cynic. Maybe they believed in divine intervention. Regardless, the church looked the same inside and outside except for the Christmas decorations and the nativity scene.

Our nativity scene was at the front of the church every Christmas. I suspect it predated my memories by fifty or more years. It looked shopworn. Mary's lips were chipped and looked chapped. Joseph's beard had worn to the extent it was now more like a goatee. And Jesus' face had been caressed so many times that the finish on His cheeks was spotted. He looked as if He had acne. In my prayers, I asked God for a new nativity scene. I also asked for forgiveness for my inappropriate thoughts about some in the congregation and our blessed family figures. I wondered to whom the church would address its letter if it wanted a new nativity scene. I wasn't sure if this was a job for God or Santa Claus.

Church and sidewalk spots held a lot in common for me. When I took time to examine them, I always found I came away with more questions than answers. Both gave me great solace. I should have been able to take comfort in church rather than my sidewalk spots. Unlike the truly faithful, I needed both in my life.

For other congregants, today was just the same as any other holiday Mass. I was sure no one around me knew my thoughts about them. I was also sure no one knew about all the questions that churned in my head. I assumed they found solace when they discovered nothing had changed since their last visit. Part of me envied them. Another part of me knew my condescension was wrong. Still, another part of me just didn't know what to think.

Mass ended. I gave thanks. I could put these thoughts aside until the next holiday Mass.

Chapter 15
Side Dish

As my mother and I walked from church to Aunt Edna's for Christmas dinner, she said, "Wasn't that a lovely Mass?"

I knew it was a rhetorical question. She didn't want to hear my real thoughts. I said, "Yes, it was lovely. I can hardly wait to get to Aunt Edna's. There's nothing better than the smell of turkey as it cooks."

"I'll fight you for a leg," she said with a smile.

"Maybe Aunt Edna won't want one, and we will have one each, so we won't have to fight." She nodded. The rest of the way, we walked in silence. We were lost in our own thoughts. I stared at my sidewalk spots. As we walked, each spot started to look like a platter. As we walked even farther, each platter looked like it held a roasted turkey. My spots made me hungry. It was Christmas Day, after all.

We arrived at Aunt Edna's building and climbed three flights of stairs to her apartment. With each step, I sniffed and expected to find a whiff of roast turkey. By the third floor, my nostrils detected a faint odor. I expected it to be stronger. We knocked on Aunt Edna's apartment door.

Then, as was her Christmas tradition, she answered, "Who goes there?"

And, as was our Christmas tradition, we shouted, "Ho, ho, ho, Merry Christmas! It's your elves bearing gifts." There were no Magi among us, just a couple of weary shepherds.

Aunt Edna embraced and kissed us as we entered her apartment. Now, the smell of turkey was a little more evident but not as strong as I remembered from Christmases past. I also realized it was still early in the day and reasoned the smell would increase as time passed.

Sometimes anticipation is as wonderful as the real thing. For example, every August I could hardly wait for the first the first day of school. But by the time the first day's dismissal bell rang, school was anticlimactic. Turkey, though, was an exception. In my opinion, nothing tastes better than turkey.

It's the only meal worth waiting twelve months to enjoy. When combined with mashed potatoes, peas, stuffing, and gravy, a turkey dinner is more splendid than any other meal. It's heavenly. For me, it's tantamount to what some would call a religious experience. I looked forward to my experience today.

As we took our customary seats in Aunt Edna's living room, she presented each of us with a glass of eggnog. This year, it tasted a little different from other years. "I put a little rum in yours, too, Marcus. Now you're just about through high school, you're old enough to have a little taste."

Out of the corner of my eye, I saw my mother lift her eyebrows, but she didn't comment. Instead, she said, "Cheers! Merry Christmas and to your good health." I'd like to say I enjoyed this year's eggnog more than other years, but I thought the rum made the eggnog smell funny. Maybe that's why the turkey smell was so faint. The eggnog also tasted bitter. If she offered me another glass, I would ask Aunt Edna to leave out the rum. I was content to be my own age. Besides, I didn't want anything to get in the way of the roast turkey smell.

"Let's open our gifts," Aunt Edna said, as if there were a huge bounty under the tree that sat on her dining room table. Aunt Edna's tree was white. Actually, it was off-white. I wasn't sure if off-white was its original color or if it had discolored with age. Regardless, it was made out of what looked to be bottle brushes. Each brush had a red, yellow, blue, or green light at the end. The tree was fixed in a small red shiny pot with some imitation moss around its base. Despite the moss, the tree looked top heavy in the small pot. I expected it to fall over any minute. Aunt Edna had placed it on a beige lace doily. I believe it was an effort on her part to make it look dignified. Unlike our tree, it had no ornaments or tinsel. Regardless, it looked festive. I am sure her tree was just as special to her as ours was to us. The gift wrap on the five parcels helped make her tree seem more colorful.

"Here's a gift addressed to you, Rita," my Aunt Edna said as she passed the gift to my mother. "Be careful—it's heavier than it looks."

My mother took the gift and then read the gift tag. "Why, it's from Marcus!" She opened each end of the parcel carefully, which was in sharp contrast to the clumsy way in which I had wrapped it with far too much cellophane sticky tape. After my mother had opened each end, she turned the parcel over and separated the paper from the center mound of tape. There was a long pause. I wasn't sure if it was because my mother didn't know what I had given her, if she didn't like it, or something else. After what seemed to be an eternity, she raised her head and said "Marcus, wherever did you find such a beautiful wooden bowl, and how could you ever afford to pay for it?" My chest swelled with pride, and I am sure my cheeks turned red, too. I told her I made the bowl in shop class. "I'm overwhelmed!" Then, my mother said something I never heard her say before or since: "I will treasure it always."

Aunt Edna broke the spell by saying, "Rita, now it's your turn to pass a gift from under the tree." My mother paused. Like me, I think she was overwhelmed, but for different reasons. I believe she wanted to enjoy the moment as much as I wanted to watch her enjoy it.

My mother walked over to the dining table, picked up another gift, read the tag, and passed it to Aunt Edna. "Why, it's from Marcus!"

exclaimed Aunt Edna. Her exclamation, like my mother's, was evidence of my new role as a gift giver. Until this year, any gifts I had ever given had been purchased by my mother and tagged under my name. Like my mother, Aunt Edna carefully opened each end of my clumsily wrapped parcel. Then, like my mother, she flipped the gift over and separated the paper from the center. Unlike my mother, she didn't pause. She picked it up, turned it around for us to see, and then said, "Just what I have always wanted, a cup holder. Thank you, Marcus." Aunt Edna seemed delighted. I was happy it was something she always wanted, except it was it wasn't a cup holder; it was supposed to be a towel holder. Apparently, my woodworking talents were not as good as I thought. My gift had cast no spell over Aunt Edna, but I was consoled by her enthusiasm.

Now it was Aunt Edna's turn again to pass out another gift. She picked up one of three left on the table. This time, the tag was addressed to me. My parcel was a rectangular box. The gift wrap was secured by red ribbon and a bow with a tiny pine cone glued in its center. The tag read, "To Marcus, love from Aunt Edna." The box was so pretty, I hesitated to open it. Like my mother and my aunt, who set the standards for how to open gifts, after I removed the ribbon, I carefully opened each end of the parcel. There was no mound of cellophane sticky tape to get in my way.

Then I flipped the parcel over and opened the gift paper at the center to reveal a shiny silver-colored cardboard box. I set aside the gift wrap. I wondered what could be inside the box. For a second, I hoped for a scarf or maybe gloves. They were items I could always use. I lifted the lid from the box. It was a leather wallet. Unlike Aunt Edna, I couldn't say, "Just what I always wanted," because I never wanted a wallet. The thought of a wallet had never crossed my mind. Why would I ever want a wallet? I had nothing to put in one. Because I didn't want to appear ungrateful, and I didn't want to embarrass my mother, I said,

"Wow! A leather wallet. It's really special. Thank you, Aunt Edna." I believe I made Aunt Edna feel good about the gift she gave me.

Sometime ago, I learned to say, "Wow" when in doubt about what to say. I figured out that a guy sometimes needs a non-confrontational word at his disposal. If he's lucky, he finds a multipurpose word that can show the right amount of enthusiasm in one situation or help diffuse another. "Wow" is one of those words. It can help a guy bridge the gap when he can't find the right response or if his facial expression betrays him. This was one of those times. "Wow" was redemptive on this Christmas Day.

I was careful with the gift wrap and box. We never wasted gift wrap. It was a hallmark of our family. Aunt Edna scooped up the bow, ribbon, and gift wrap no sooner than I put the pieces down. She took the little pine cone off the bow and set it aside on the little table next to her along with the bow. Then, as if it were the most natural thing to do, she took the ribbon and straightened it from one to end to the other. Yet this wasn't enough. Aunt Edna took the ribbon in her right hand and went on to wrap it around the index and middle fingers of her left hand. When she had created a roll of ribbon, she set it next to the bow in her neat little row of Christmas gift residue. Next came the gift paper. She picked it up, put it on her lap, and flattened it as best she could. As she did so, she looked up and said, "I'll iron it later." She picked up the silver box last and placed the pine cone, bow, and roll of ribbon inside. Then, she covered them with the silver box lid. She put it on top of the gift paper. I have no idea how Aunt Edna planned to reuse any of these. Rest assured that I would be on the lookout for them next Christmas. Aunt Edna didn't try to flatten the gift paper I had used on my gifts, nor did she try to unravel and reroll the mound of sticky cellophane tape that stuck to it. I wasn't offended. I would try to do better next year.

Now it was my turn. I picked up one of two gifts left. I picked the one with a bow and a little star glued in its center. The tag said, "To

Rita, love from Edna." While I presented the gift to my mother, Aunt Edna stood up abruptly and said, "I have to check on the turkey and turn the heat on the vegetables if we plan on eating any time soon." Her words were music to my ears. My mother waited for her to return before she opened her gift. This was another standard set by the Hanlon sisters. We had to wait until everyone was present for presents.

While we waited, I tried to get a sniff of the turkey as Aunt Edna opened the oven door. I was disappointed. The smell didn't seem to be any stronger than when we arrived. Maybe my nose had become used to it. But there was no need to despair. The turkey would be done soon enough. In a little while, we would sit and enjoy the best meal of the year.

Just as before, my mother carefully removed the bow and ribbon. She handed them immediately to Aunt Edna. I wasn't sure why the giver got the gift wrap and its embellishments rather than the givee. I wasn't going to ask. It was just another one of the Hanlon sisters' long list of gift practices. Still, I wondered if this same ritual happened in other families on Christmas Day.

Another one of the Hanlon sisters' rituals was how to open a gift. My mother and Aunt Edna elevated this practice to an art form. In accordance with their standards, my mother opened each end of her parcel. Then, she flipped the parcel over, opened the gift paper, and revealed a shiny silver paper box. She handed Aunt Edna the gift wrapping.

The Hanlon sisters had no standards for gift reactions. For them, unlike me, their reactions were spontaneous. "Why, Edna, it's beautiful. It must have cost you a fortune. The colors are so beautiful." I heard no hesitation is my mother's voice and saw no betrayal in her facial expression. She grinned from ear to ear. Her voice matched her face. No "wow" came from her lips. Either she really liked what she received, or she was a consummate liar. I wondered what was in the silver rectangle box. I heard the word "fortune." Could it be money? Could it be a check? Could it be a piece of jewelry? As these questions whirled around in my head, I realized my questions were like the ones Nobby asked. Not a good sign. My mother lifted the gift out of the silver box. It was a scarf. It was pretty, but it was just a scarf. My mother put it around her neck, and without hesitation, she went on to say, "The colors are perfect, and it's so soft. Thank you, Edna."

Now it was my mother's turn. She picked up the last gift. This one was rectangular, too. It was nicely wrapped and surrounded by green ribbon rather than red. This package had no bow. My mother handed the present to her sister. Aunt Edna looked at the gift tag and read aloud, "To Edna, with love from your sister Rita." I wondered why my mother wrote "sister." As far as I knew, Aunt Edna was my mother's only sister.

Like my mother, Aunt Edna carefully removed the ribbon. She held it up and attempted to straighten it by running it between her thumb and index finger. As before, she took one end and rolled it over her index and middle fingers. Then she opened the silver box and placed the green ribbon roll next to the red ribbon roll, the tiny pine cone, and the little star. Once she finished all procedures to her satisfaction, Aunt Edna opened each end of the parcel, flipped it over, opened the gift paper, and revealed a white box. It looked to be the same size as the silver boxes my mother and I received from Aunt Edna and forfeited to her. Aunt Edna lifted the lid of the white box. "What a surprise. Rita, you have excellent taste."

This time, I detected hesitation in Aunt Edna's voice and the look on her face didn't match what she said. Her face had also turned red. What could it all mean? I waited to hear her say, "Wow," but it didn't come. Aunt Edna lifted her gift from the white box. My mother smiled.

Actually, she beamed. Lo and behold, my mother had given Aunt Edna the same scarf Aunt Edna had given my mother. For me, it was definite "wow" moment. Unlike me, Aunt Edna didn't seem to have a multi-purpose word at her disposal. I could tell she was nonplussed. For my mother, I guessed this was a triumphant moment. Except for the color of the box, she had matched Aunt Edna. For Aunt Edna, I sensed this was a moment of humility. Her sister had matched her, gift for gift. Although Aunt Edna had kept both silver boxes, she now asked my mother if she wanted the white box back so she could keep her scarf in it. My mother didn't miss a beat. "No, Edna, I plan to wear my scarf home. You can keep the box along with the silver ones."

Aunt Edna rose quickly. I wondered if she wanted to escape. She went into the kitchen while my mother and I enjoyed another glass of eggnog. This time, I asked for no rum. I liked the taste better. It was much sweeter and not the least bit bitter. While we sat, I heard sounds I interpreted to be the sounds of potatoes being drained and mashed. I also thought I heard the sound of gravy being stirred. I still didn't detect a strong turkey scent. Just then, Aunt Edna shouted, "It won't be long." A few minutes later, she returned with placemats and cutlery.

"Do you want me to set the table?" asked my mother.

"No, I have everything under control," Aunt Edna replied.

Aunt Edna set a placemat down in front of each of the three chairs at her dining table. The placements were patterned with Christmas trees. Then she placed each dinner napkin, which had the same pattern as the placemats, on the left. Next she placed the cutlery on each placemat. The cutlery consisted of two types of forks—a large one and a small one. They were placed vertically on the left-hand side of each placemat; a knife was placed vertically near the right side. Two types of spoons—a round one and an elliptical one—completed the setting.

The round one was placed horizontally near the top of each placemat, and the elliptical was placed vertically to the right of each knife.

While she set the table, Aunt Edna remarked she had prepared something different for this year's Christmas dinner. "Usually, I shop at Safeway or Park and Shop, but last week I decided to go to Petrini's Market for the turkey. As you know, their meat department is the best. Because Christmas is such a special occasion, I wanted to get something special for us. So I hope you enjoy this year's turkey."

My mother and I raised our eyebrows in puzzlement. We both knew Petrini's offered a cut above, both figuratively and literally, when it came to meat. Today would be our first taste. My mother didn't shop there because she believed it was beyond her budget. From time to time, we would walk by Petrini's and she would always say, "The Nobs buy their food here."

My mouth watered. Not only would I get to eat the best meal of the year, but I would also eat the best food of the city and of my life to date. I could hardly wait. Aunt Edna went on, "Rather than put all the serving dishes and platters on the table, we'll have a buffet, and you can serve yourselves."

My day was getting better and better. If I could beat my mother to the front of our short line, I was sure to get a drumstick. Time couldn't go fast enough for me. If I had known about the Petrini's turkey, I would have offered to set the table for Aunt Edna to speed things along. However, I am certain the napkins and cutlery would not have made it to her exact and neatly appointed positions, which in Aunt Edna's mind, would have jeopardized dinner. No, today, I would just have to bide my time like a good guest until Aunt Edna was ready for us. The wait was painful. Finally, Aunt Edna called us to come to the kitchen. My mother and I stood up together.

Her smile was as wide as mine. However, she was closest to the door, so she made it to the kitchen first. I didn't despair. After all, every turkey has two legs. I could see Aunt Edna stand back to let my mother and me go before her. Yes, I could feel it. Today was the day of my dreams. What could be better than a roast turkey leg on Christmas Day?

My mother picked up a plate. As she did so, I could see her scan all the bowls before her. Her smile remained intact, which was a good sign. Maybe she would decide against a turkey leg and leave both for me. I thought my head would explode at the prospect. I wanted to yell, "Hurry up!" but knew my mother was as anxious for her dinner as I was for mine.

From my perch just outside the kitchen door, I saw her pick up a roll, a scoop of mashed potatoes, half a spoonful of peas, and a full spoonful of cheese-covered cauliflower. From my vantage point, I couldn't see the turkey or the gravy boat, so I couldn't tell which piece my mother was going to choose.

Just then, my mother's whole expression changed. Her smile disappeared, her eyebrows furrowed, and her head pulled back like she had seen a train wreck. "What the hell is this?" she gasped. What had caused her reaction? Was it a roach? Was it a mouse? It had to be something serious. My mother was seldom surprised by anything. After all, she worked in a bar in the Tenderloin. She had already seen about all the nasty stuff there was to see. I thrust my head in the doorway. I had to find out.

It was neither a roach nor a mouse. It was something worse. On the turkey platter lay a beige and brown object. It looked like a football without the points at the ends. I thought Aunt Edna had discovered some new type of vegetable or mushroom concoction at Petrini's. I continued to stare. All of a sudden, I heard Aunt Edna proclaim this thing, this ugly object that glistened under the kitchen light and shook slightly when my mother poked it, was a turkey roll. "They're something new," extolled Aunt Edna. "While they're more expensive than a traditional turkey, these have no bones, so there's no waste. I am excited to have you try it."

By the look on my mother's face, I thought she might faint. All I could say was, "Wow."

My mother took a slice of turkey roll and smothered it with gravy. I sensed she was trying to cover it up just as a coroner would cover up a dead body at a crime scene. By the angle at which she held her head, I could tell my mother was afraid to look at it any longer than necessary. Because she applied more gravy than ever, I knew my mother was equally afraid of how it would taste.

My spirits were so crushed, I didn't want to eat. I was so desolate that I didn't hear Ant Edna say it was my turn. It wasn't until she asked loudly, "Marcus, are you okay?" that I snapped out of my despair. I took my cue from my mother and filled my plate the same way she had filled hers. I took one slice of the mystery meat and covered it with gravy. "Is that all you're having, Marcus?" Aunt Edna asked.

"For now," I mumbled.

The three of us sat around the table. Neither my mother nor I said a word as we tried to eat what was supposed to be the best meal of the year. In the background, I could hear Aunt Edna as she chattered away, but I wasn't in any mood to listen. Instead, I worked around the other items of my plate while I waited for my mother to take her first bite of the turkey roll. There was no need for me to be the guinea pig, I thought. If she didn't gag, choke, or fall off her chair, I would try it, too. I watched as my mother cut a small piece. She said, "Please pass the cranberry sauce." Good idea, I thought.

If the gravy didn't cover the taste of the turkey roll, the cranberries offered an extra layer of protection. My mother stuck her fork into the small piece of turkey roll and with her knife placed a small amount of potatoes and cranberry sauce on top. She lifted the fork to her mouth.

She seemed to take forever. Finally, she opened her mouth and put her fork in. She closed her lips over the fork and slid it out of her mouth. She chewed. She swallowed. I could hardly wait for her verdict. "Not bad, Edna," she said. Not bad! My mother's face gave her away. I could tell she hated it. Why did she pull her punches? My mother and Aunt Edna could fight with the best of them. If my mother had quaffed a few beers instead of sips of eggnog, she would have told Aunt Edna the truth. Or, maybe in the spirit of Christmas my mother gave Aunt Edna a pass.

I ate my dinner, too, and didn't say a word. I now knew why I could hardly smell roast turkey all afternoon. It wasn't a real turkey, despite Aunt Edna's claims to the contrary. For the first time ever, I didn't have seconds. I didn't even want dessert.

After my mother helped Aunt Edna clear the table and wash the dishes, she said, "It's probably time for us to go. I've got to be at work by midnight." As she spoke, my mother grabbed our coats off Aunt Edna's bed. She wrapped her new scarf around her neck.

"I thought you might save your scarf for good," said Aunt Edna.

My mother stood straighter and replied, "What could be better than now as I walk home with my son on Christmas?" As I buttoned my coat, one of those pesky little lumps got stuck in my throat. With a few words, my mother made up for a disastrous Christmas Day.

We began our walk home. For the first couple of blocks, neither of us said a word. All of a sudden, my mother exclaimed, "What the hell was all that? I don't care what she says—Edna didn't get that thing from Petrini's. Who's she trying to fool? I wouldn't even sole my shoes with that thing. And goodness knows I wouldn't bother to save it for sandwiches." She laughed and laughed like I had never heard her laugh before. She made me laugh, too. Through peals of laughter, she went on to say, "I've seen better-looking pigeons in Union Square than whatever it was your Aunt Edna was trying to pass off as a turkey."

"I know," I chortled. "I saw a really fat one in front of the St. Francis Hotel the other day. It would have been a whole lot tastier."

Then my mother surprised me and asked, "Was it one of the flock that sits on the canopy over the entryway? Because they are really fat."

She was in such a good mood, I couldn't resist and said, "No, Mom, it was on the sidewalk and carried a protest sign. It said, 'Ban the Bomb and Turkey Roll.'"

My mother laughed so hard that tears ran down her cheeks. Soon, we were both convulsed with laughter. I didn't think it was possible, but we laughed even more. My sides hurt. "That's one for the books," declared my mother. We walked and walked some more. Eventually, our laughter subsided and we lapsed into silence once again. Neither of us said a word until we reached our building. As my mother opened the door to our apartment, she pulled off her scarf, dropped her shoulders, sighed, and whispered, "Merry Christmas Marcus. Thank you."

Chapter 16
Side Glances

Before I knew it, January was over. February passed with little to mark its passage except the ash cross on my forehead to mark the start of Lent. Spring was around the corner. Thanks to Mary Ellen, my grades were good. Sometime in March, our school guidance counselor, Mr. Johnstone, started to meet with all the senior students. My turn came on the first day of spring, March twenty-first.

"What are your plans after you graduate?" Mr. Johnstone asked in an authoritative voice. His manner suggested I should have a good answer. Unfortunately, I did not.

"Mr. Johnstone," I started.

He corrected me. "It's pronounced like 'John son,' not 'John stone.' The 't' is silent."

I wished I could have been silent, too. Nonetheless, I told him I just wanted to improve my grades. I had not yet given thought as to what I might do after high school graduation. The look on his face told me mine wasn't the response he expected to hear.

"Marcus, based on your reports, I see your grades have indeed improved since the fall. So, I am perplexed. Why haven't you thought about college? Your grades certainly qualify you to apply. Why did you work so hard to improve your grades if you don't have any aspirations toward higher education?"

I explained to Mr. Johnstone the cost of college tuition was beyond me or my mother. I improved my grades so I could graduate from high school. More importantly, I hoped better grades might help me find a better a job right after graduation so I could lighten my mother's load. As I spoke, Mr. Johnstone nodded his head. I wasn't sure if it was because he understood, he sympathized, or he had a spastic neck.

While Mr. Johnstone pondered, I looked around his office. One wall was covered with what appeared to be twelve or thirteen diplomas and certificates. The principal didn't have as many certificates on his office wall. The few times I was in the principal's office, the most I saw three—two diplomas from two different universities and one from a teacher's college. In Mr. Johnstone's office, the print was too small on any of the certificates for me to read them. As a result, I couldn't tell where they were from or what they represented, except all were neatly and uniformly framed in black. They hung evenly in three rows behind his desk. It was obvious all were important to him because of the way they were framed and hung. It made me wonder what he had done to earn them. Before I could ask, Mr. Johnstone asked, "Have you ever thought about a plan that would allow you to work full time plus attend college as a part-time student?" The truth was that such a plan had never crossed my mind because I didn't know that there was one. I told him so.

Mr. Johnstone sat up straighter in his chair, leaned forward, and clasped his hands together. "Marcus, is this an option you would like to pursue?"

I sat up straighter, too. My unhelmeted head felt as if it had just been tackled by a linebacker in the end zone. The thought of a job and a college education at the same time appealed to me. It also overwhelmed me. I stammered until what seemed to be the longest "yes" ever uttered finally came out of my mouth.

"Great!" Mr. Johnstone cried. "Then let's get started." I was glad he knew where to begin, because I didn't have a clue.

Now I started to understand why Mr. Johnstone had so many certificates on his wall. Then, in what seemed to be spoken in a one long breath, he said, "I see you do well in mathematics, Marcus. Why don't we find you a position in insurance where you can put those skills to work? San Francisco has several insurance companies where I have contacts. We'll find you a position with one of them. At the same time, we'll start the application process for you to attend Golden Gate University on a part-time basis. It offers classes in insurance. Those classes would you help you get ahead in your new career. We'll also see about tuition assistance, either through the university or through your new employer. Come back to my office in three days and I should have everything put together for you."

How did he come up with this plan so quickly? I felt as if I were drowning in a sea of new ideas and didn't know how to swim. Yet Mr. Johnstone rattled off ideas automatically, as if it were an everyday occurrence. In less than an hour, I had gone from a student who just wanted to graduate from high school to one who could have a career and higher education at the same time. Whew! What would tell my mother? Would she even believe me? I could hardly believe what had just happened. Had it really happened?

I decided to wait until I met with Mr. Johnstone again before I said anything to anyone. Then I hoped I would come away with a better handle on whether any of his ideas were going to become a reality. I didn't want to raise my mother's expectations or mine unnecessarily. I also wanted to come to terms with everything he laid out before me. First of all, I needed time to find out more about insurance. Apart from what little I gleaned from billboards and a few television advertisements, I knew nothing about insurance except it was as solid as the rock of Gibraltar.

Even though I had no career plans, was a career in insurance one I wanted to pursue? I did know that insurance companies employ lots of people. If I walked by the Transamerica building during the late afternoon, I would see people stream out of it and run to catch buses or trains. What made them decide to work for an insurance company? Was I going to be a part of this swarm of people? Did I want to be part of it? I wondered if any of them took part-time college classes. I suspected the men in suits had already attended university and held degrees. That's why they could afford to dress so well. It was a lot for me to take in. Even so, I desperately wanted it all to be true. The idea I could wear a suit and a pair of hard-soled shoes every day was something I had never dreamed about until now. While I didn't know much about insurance companies, I was certain no insurance company employee laced up a pair of high-top Converse canvas shoes every morning before setting off for a day's work. For the first time, I saw a future, and it included more than one pair of brown hard-soled shoes.

During the next three days, I found it difficult to concentrate in any of my classes. I focused on my sidewalk spots and hoped they would help me find answers to my questions. While their constancy gave me comfort, for the first time, they let me down. No supernatural phoenixes rose out of them to burn away my confusion, nor did they give me any clarity.

My next appointment with Mr. Johnstone came around. I used the excuse slip he had given me during our last meeting. When I presented the slip to the teacher, she simply nodded her head. As I started to leave the classroom, a few of the students whispered. Nobby muttered under his breath. His tone suggested something nefarious: "I wonder what he did?" I smiled. Compared to Nobby, I was an angel. Compared to Nobby, all students were angels. For him to suggest I might be in some sort of trouble was ironic, to say the least. I was sure he spent more time in the principal's office than the principal.

While I walked to Mr. Johnstone's office, I wondered what Nobby would do after he graduated from high school. I also wondered if Mr. Johnstone had come up with a plan for him. It would take a man with at least twelve certificates and diplomas to come up with a career path for Nobby. Some might argue it would take a judge and jury to make him find his way in the world. However, today wasn't about Nobby's future. Today was about mine.

When I reached Mr. Johnstone's office, I could see him through the window in his door. His attention was focused on a pile of papers. I wondered if those papers concerned me. His brow was furrowed. The fingers of his right hand held a pen, which wobbled. The fingers of his left hand rubbed at his chin. I didn't want to disturb him even though I had an appointment. I tapped on the door. He dropped his pen and motioned for me to come into his office. Once I entered, he told me to sit and make myself comfortable. He collected the papers on his desk and moved them to one side. How could I possibly be comfortable when my future was in those hands? I tried not to show my nervousness. Instead, I thanked him. Would this magic word make a difference today? While I tried not to expect too much, I hoped Mr. Johnstone would pull the proverbial rabbit out of the hat for me today.

"Marcus, I have wonderful news for you. I have been in touch with my contacts. They were impressed with the improvement in your academic performance and would like to offer you a position in their claims department when you graduate. Additionally, they are prepared to help you attend Golden Gate University. The company will subsidize a portion of your tuition. Upon satisfactory completion of each course, the company will reimburse you for your portion of the cost. I have their offer letter, which I hope you will review with your mother and accept. This is an excellent opportunity for you, Marcus. Do you have any questions?"

Mr. Johnstone said all of this quickly and in one big breath. After I heard him say, "Wonderful news," I found it difficult to take it all in. All my worries over the past three days evaporated. I could hardly wait to get home and tell my mother the good news.

Questions! Sure, I had a million of them. For now, though, I was still trying to take everything in. I took some deep breaths. "May I ask you the name of the company?"

"Yes, Marcus. It's Transamerica. Anything else?"

"No, Mr. Johnstone. Not right now. Thank you so much, sir, for all your help. I won't let you down."

"Marcus, I have confidence in you, and I hope you'll come back and see me once you are settled in your new job. Now, here's a hall pass to return to your class."

I didn't want to go back to class. I wanted to run through the halls and yell, "I got a job! I'm going to college!" Unfortunately, I still had two more classes to attend before the end of the school day.

I entered English class, handed the teacher the hall pass, and took my seat. Not a word was exchanged between the teacher and me. Once again, I could hear the whispers of a few students. Once again, Nobby muttered, "I wonder what he did?" Until I shared the news with my mother, they would just have to wonder.

Chapter 17
Walk Tall

Most kids would have been able to share their good news with their
parents over dinner or at least some during the same day. For me,
it was different. My mother got home long after I was asleep, and
I didn't want to disturb her sleep when I was awake. I hoped my
mother would recognize the great opportunity Mr. Johnstone had
found for me. I also knew my mother could be difficult. The degree to
which she might be difficult could also depend on the day of the week
and the voice in her head. As I got older, my mother's voices bothered
me less. I believe it was partly because I became more used to them
and partly because I became more independent.

For my mother, Saturday and Sunday were always better days than
the rest. I didn't know if I could hold my news until Sunday when I
knew she would be at her best. I decided to take the risk and share
the letter with her on Saturday morning after she finished her Friday
night shift. She would be exhausted, but she would have the next day
to sleep and regroup.

I set my alarm for 5:30 A.M. to be up, washed, dressed, and ready
when my mother got home. When she got home, she often brewed a
pot of coffee before she headed off to sleep. As she sipped her coffee
and waited for me to get up so she could take the bed, she would read
yesterday's *Chronicle*. Tomorrow, I would be up and would make the
coffee for her.

Saturday morning came, and I got up to make coffee. The problem
was that I wasn't sure how to make a pot, although I had watched my
mother do it many times. I grabbed the metal coffee pot, filled it with

water, and placed it on the stove burner, which I turned to "high." Then I took the metal basket and put in two scoops of coffee from the tin above the stove. It didn't look like quite enough, so I added two more scoops. I returned the basket filled with coffee back to the pot, put on the lid with the clear glass top knob, and waited for the coffee to percolate. I knew once the coffee started to look brown as it rose to the top of the glass knob, it would be done and the burner could be turned down to "low." I had just turned the burner down when my mother walked through our apartment door.

"I hope that coffee tastes as good as it smells," she said. I hoped so, too. "To what do I owe this pleasure?" I told my mother that I had something to discuss with her. "What have you done?" For a stupid second, I thought my mother had spoken to Nobby. Why did everyone assume I must have done something wrong? It wasn't my nature to misbehave. I told my mother I had done nothing wrong. Instead, I told her I had some good news about my future. "Future!" she yelped as if someone had poked her with a fork. "Who around here has any future?" Perhaps Saturday morning wasn't a good time to share my news after all. But it was too late. I was committed.

As I served her a cup of coffee, I put the letter Mr. Johnstone had given to me in front of her and asked her to read it. I was worried she might opt for the *Chronicle* first, but she opened the letter and started to read. Her face did not betray her. I couldn't tell if she understood the letter, if she didn't care, if she was surprised, or something else. Finally, she looked up and asked, "What does all this mean, Marcus?"

I explained that right after my graduation, I would start a career in insurance at Transamerica. My weekly salary would be $155.00, and I would also get benefits. Additionally, I would enroll in insurance classes at Golden Gate University as a part-time student. The company would help me with my college expenses.

As I spoke, my mother had her head in her hands. Each thumb was either side of her chin, and her fingers were splayed against each side of her forehead. After I finished, she put down her hands, raised her head, grabbed her cup, and took another sip of coffee. "Marcus, that's more money than I make." I couldn't tell by her facial expression if she was pleased. After many minutes, she spoke. "I think we need to call your Aunt Edna and ask her to come over. Then we will tell her the good news together. Maybe we'll all share a few beers. Meanwhile, I'm going to bed. Thanks for the coffee. It was good."

I don't know what I expected from my mother. I didn't expect hosannas, but I hoped for a smile or some congratulatory words. I sensed she liked the coffee more than the contents of my letter. Yet the fact she wanted my Aunt Edna to come over later meant she was anxious to share the news. My mother's joy would probably depend on the level of Aunt Edna's enthusiasm. If so, I needn't worry. Aunt Edna was my biggest fan. After a few beers and a heavy dose of Aunt Edna, I was confident my mother would think I was presidential material. She would sign the letter and I could return it to Mr. Johnstone on Monday morning.

Aunt Edna arrived around four o'clock. My mother was still in bed, but once she heard Aunt Edna's voice, she called out from the bedroom: "I'll be right with you." She also asked me to put on a pot of coffee. Things started to look up. She must have liked my coffee. I made my second pot.

About fifteen minutes later, my mother sauntered into our kitchen. She was still in her bathrobe, but I could tell she had washed her face and combed her hair. She took the last seat at the table. While she did so, I got up and poured her a cup of coffee. "Did Marcus tell you our news?" So it was our news now. She was a part of it, which was another good sign.

"What news?" asked Aunt Edna.

"Go ahead and tell her, Marcus," my mother said.

After I explained everything to Aunt Edna, my mother said, "Show her the letter."

Aunt Edna took the envelope from me, extracted the letter, and started to read. Unlike my mother, her face lit up. The more she read, the more she smiled. When she finished, Aunt Edna folded the letter, put it back in the envelope, and clapped her hands. "This is the most exciting news that's ever happened to our family since the day you were born, Marcus!"

My mother nodded. "Isn't it great news, Edna?"

I had just hit a two-run homer. Then my mother said, "Let's sign the letter before anyone changes their mind at that Transamerica place. And let's have a beer to celebrate."

I passed on the beer. My mother and Aunt Edna enjoyed their first, second, and third as I never had seen them enjoy beer before. While they drank, they reminisced. They talked about when construction began on the Transamerica building and how, when it was finished, it changed the San Francisco skyline. Both agreed that it took some time to get used to a pyramid, and they remembered how everyone joked that it was for a skinny pharaoh. They also agreed that their parents wouldn't like San Francisco today. It had so many more people and was much busier. Most of all, they agreed that both of their parents would be proud of me, especially if I got a college education. I would be the first in my family to do so.

I wondered why they thought I would want to impress people I didn't even know or care about. My grandparents had rejected my mother and me before I was born. They hadn't even crossed my mind. I simply wanted to impress my mother and Aunt Edna. I hoped I wouldn't let them down.

While was lost in my thoughts, I heard Aunt Edna suggest we celebrate. For a moment, I thought she meant Mass, but then I heard her tack on "My treat." It would have been an equally good idea for me to attend Mass and give thanks for my good fortune. I would give thanks tomorrow.

Today, we would celebrate over a nice dinner. We headed for Lefty O'Doul's.

Some may not have considered Lefty's a posh restaurant, but for us, it was nirvana. As we grabbed our trays and went slowly down the line, the smells of turkey, roast beef, gravy, and mashed potatoes were heavenly. I liked how they sliced roast turkey. It came from a real turkey, not a turkey roll. They also added as much gravy as I wanted. Lefty O'Doul's offered lots of choices and large portions. Aunt Edna paid while my mother and I looked for a table. We found one close to the back. After we set our trays down, Aunt Edna went to the bar and bought two beers, one for her and one for my mother. This time, she didn't offer me one. Although I was still too young to drink alcohol, I was old enough to get a full-time job and go to college at the same time.

While we savored our dinners, Aunt Edna brought the conversation around to clothes. I had no idea where she was headed. By the look on my mother's face, she didn't know, either. "You can't go off to work at an insurance company wearing those dungarees and plaid shirts. You'll have to get yourself a suitable wardrobe. If you want to get ahead, you'll have to make a good impression." I knew what Aunt Edna meant, but for tonight, I just wanted to enjoy my roast turkey.

My mother sighed. "Edna's right. We'll have to get you some new clothes, although I'm not sure how we'll pay for them or how we'll get you fitted."

Without batting an eye, Aunt Edna laid out her plan. We would watch for sales at J.C. Penney. Then we would go and get me fitted for some grey flannels, white shirts, and a navy blue blazer. As usual, Aunt Edna imposed her sense of style.

I didn't recall anyone in a navy blue blazer or grey flannels when I saw them exit the insurance company. Instead, I saw grey suits and navy blue suits. Most suits were plain, although a few had pinstripes. I sensed this kind of wardrobe would do more to help me get ahead than Aunt Edna's kind. I didn't say a word. I just continued to eat my roast turkey. I would speak to my mother later, and together we would figure out what I needed to get me started and how to pay for it. I would also ask Mr. Johnstone for his advice. Then I knew we would start our search where we always started our searches, at the Goodwill store.

Monday morning, I returned the signed letter to Mr. Johnstone and thanked him, once again, for all his help. "Don't mention it," he said, but I knew he wanted me to mention it because I saw his chest expand as I expressed my gratitude.

"Mr. Johnstone, do you have any advice for me about the types of clothes I should buy? I want to look my best for this job."

He didn't let me down. "First off, buy yourself a navy blue suit along with four or five white shirts, black shoes, black socks, and a few neckties. Invest in a grey suit later, after you make some money. With different colored neckties, you can change the entire look of your appearance, even though you may have only one suit. Let me check my closet; I may have some neckties to get you started." Once again, Mr. Johnstone came to my rescue.

In addition to my career plan, I now had a wardrobe plan to help me get ahead. I now knew why Mr. Johnstone had so many certificates on his wall. Each one probably recognized each student he helped. I wish I had a certificate to give him. But I suspected Mr. Johnstone took greater pleasure in his students' successes than he did in any certificate or award. I wouldn't let him down. He didn't let me down, either. A few days later, while I changed classes, Mr. Johnstone motioned me to come over. He handed me a brown paper bag and said, "Here's some ties for you."

Chapter 18
Side Show

My classmates wanted to know what was in the brown paper bag. I just smiled and said that I would let them know during our lunch period. Nobby was undeterred and demanded "Tell me now." I shook my head. He would have to wait like everyone else.

Mary Ellen shrugged her shoulders. "Okay, then. We'll wait."

I'm sure English class was interminable for Nobby, Mary Ellen, and my other classmates. They stared at me as they tried to get a clue about the bag's contents. In a weird way, I was flattered that the class was so interested in something I stashed under my desk with my books. I thought of a line from our tenth-grade English class when we studied Henry IV, Part II: "Uneasy lies the head that wears the crown." Today, it was an uneasy hand that carried a brown paper bag.

How was I going to explain a bag of neckties? More importantly, how was I going to explain why I needed neckties?

The neckties and the stares were distractions I tried to ignore as I listened to our teacher's exhortations about Shakespeare's Macbeth. We had finally reached the part in the play where the assassins kill Banquo. I suspected it was the beginning of the end for Macbeth. I liked this play a whole lot better than Henry IV, Part II. To this day, I don't know why we studied Henry IV, Part II, and didn't study Henry IV, Part I. It would have made more sense to start with Part I and then follow with Part II. Sometimes, our school curriculum made no sense to me.

Class ended. As we headed to our next one, Nobby caught up with me. "So what's in the bag?" I walked a little faster and tried to ignore him, with the hope that he would get the message and leave me alone. No dice. Nobby persisted. "I mean it, Marcus. What's in the bag?" I repeated that I would explain everything during lunch. "You'd better, or else," was all I heard him say as we entered our next class. Nobby had issued threats before. This time, his tone of voice was more sinister. He had also called me Marcus rather than Playdough. Nobby meant business. His attitude troubled me so much that for the entire next period, I was hard pressed to focus on math equations. Instead, I wondered what "or else" meant to Nobby. He left me feeling uncomfortable about something that, in reality, was none of his business. The ring of the bell ended class. It was time for lunch.

On my way to the cafeteria, I dropped my books and the paper bag off at my locker. As I placed the paper bag on the top shelf of my locker, I suddenly realized I could tell Nobby anything now that the bag was safely tucked away. But what would I tell him? Whatever I made up had to be plausible, especially to someone like Nobby. As a skillful liar himself, he could always detect a lie from someone else, like me. It was a skill I didn't possess. On the way to the cafeteria, I decided now wasn't the time to develop it. It was always better to tell the truth.

I got in line. Today, the main dish was meatloaf or "mystery meat," as we called it. I'm not sure what was in it, but I liked the taste, especially when it was smothered in gravy. It was accompanied by mashed potatoes and kernel corn, which were two more of my favorites. As I reached the end of the line, I picked up a carton of milk, placed it on my tray, and paid the cashier. I looked around for a place to sit. I needn't have bothered. Nobby waved his hands. He had set aside a place for me next to him.

I don't know why I felt as if I were walking toward the gallows. I had so much to celebrate. Yet I sensed Nobby would turn my good news into something he could deride and mock. He had become that kind of guy, one I wanted to avoid. I'm sure he still had his followers, but I wasn't one of them. I'm sure Nobby hadn't noticed. I'm sure he hadn't noticed that Rusty wasn't one of them, either. He wasn't self aware enough to notice those kinds of changes. As long as he had followers of any stripe, Nobby assumed he was king. No one told him differently. Why upset him and make trouble for ourselves?

Before I could even feel the cold metal of the seat, I heard, "So what's in the bag?" I sighed. Despite my good intentions, I lied and said it was my lunch that I had left on Mr. Johnstone's desk. "Yeah, right," said Nobby. "Then why aren't you eating it instead of mystery meat?" He wasn't buying my explanation. By the looks of their faces, the other guys weren't buying it, either.

So I told the truth. "It's a bag of neckties."

"Yeah, right. You expect us to believe you?" I told them that they could believe whatever they wanted, but the bag contained neckties. "What do you need neckties for? You don't even have a neck. Your chin sits on your chest." The guys laughed.

For the first time, I didn't care what Nobby said about me. I decided to tell them everything. The best Nobby could come up with when I finished was "Who would be dumb enough to give you a job?" It was pointless to continue. Once I graduated, I knew Nobby and I would travel different paths. Although we had a lot of history that tied us together forever, we wouldn't make any new history. We finished our lunches in silence. From time to time, Nobby stared at me for a few moments. He had nothing more to say to me. This, too, was a first.

At the end of the day, while I stood at my locker, Mary Ellen came up to me. "I'm not sure if what I heard is true, but if it is, I am so happy for you, Marcus." I asked her what she had heard, and I was surprised by the accuracy of her version. The guys had paid attention, after all.

"What you've heard is true. Thanks, Mary Ellen. Because of you, my grades got better and I became eligible for this program. In my wildest dreams, I never thought I would leave school with a job to go to and the chance for a college education."

As we spoke, we walked down the hallway and out the front door. "Marcus, I have always liked and believed in you. Everyone just needs a chance."

I hadn't felt the lump in my throat in a long while. It came back. I could barely speak. "What are going to do after graduation, Mary Ellen?" I had my fingers crossed. I hoped she would stay in San Francisco. I wanted to remain close to Mary Ellen. She had become my touchstone.

"Marcus, I am so excited! Mr. Johnstone just told me that I have been accepted and have won a scholarship. I'm going to Santa Clara University." Although my heart dropped, I was truly happy for Mary Ellen. At least she would be close to San Francisco. She could come home for holidays and special events. Once I started to work, perhaps I could afford to visit her if she invited me.

Mary Ellen and I continued to walk in the direction of her apartment. As we reached its entryway and we were about ready to say our goodbyes, Mary Ellen winked and said, "Now that you have a necktie, you can go to the prom." Before I could collect my thoughts, she ran up the stairs to her apartment.

Prom? Prom? What did Mary Ellen mean? Was that an invitation? Did she want me, Marcus Hanlon, to take her to the prom? I didn't know what to think. Somehow, though, I knew Mary Ellen expected me to ask her. At least I hoped she expected me to ask her. Wow. I would need a new suit more than ever. What a day this had been. My future changed in ways I could never have imagined just a few weeks ago.

Nobby's crack about my neck and chin got my attention. He had a point. My body parts tended to roll into one and congregate closest to my torso. I looked roly-poly. I knew I could improve my appearance. A necktie was a nice accessory, but that's all it was. I decided right then and there it was time to work on me. If I could improve my grades, I could improve my physique. I couldn't make myself any taller, but I could make myself slimmer. From now on, I would walk faster to and from school. Although a faster walk would mean less time with my sidewalk spots, it could mean a trimmer me. I could forsake my spots for a while. I didn't need any gravy on my mashed potatoes, either. I could forsake it, too. I could do it.

Chapter 19
Hotspot

I was determined to ask Mary Ellen to the prom and to lose weight. While it wouldn't cost me any money to lose weight, it would cost more than I had in my wallet to take Mary Ellen to the prom. So, on top of everything else, I needed to make some money. The Christmas money from Aunt Edna and the few coins I got from her boyfriends were not enough. I couldn't ask my mother for prom money. She had already committed what precious little she had to buy me a suit. Anyway, I wasn't after a handout. I was after a job. How ironic. In June, I would start a new job. It would pay me well. Now, though, I had no income.

While I walked back and forth to school, I checked all the store windows for help wanted signs. For the first few days, I saw none. Finally, I saw one posted in a restaurant bar window at the corner of Powell and Green Streets. I patted down my hair, hiked up my pants, walked through the swinging doors, and told the man behind the bar that I would like to apply for the job posted in the window.

While he continued to wipe the glass in his hand, the bartender tipped his head to his left and said, "See Joe." By Joe, I assumed he meant the man who sat on a stool at the end of the bar. He wore a brown suit, but it was unlike any I had seen before. The jacket didn't have lapels.

Instead, it looked more like a shirt or something I had seen Sammy Davis Jr. or the prime minster of India wear on television. The fabric was different, too. It was not like anything I had seen before. It had a pattern that looked like bumps on top of the cloth. These bumps reminded me of my sidewalk spots. Unlike my spots, which were different sizes and shapes, the bumps on this suit were all the same pattern and color. The lower sleeves of the jacket also had what looked to be snags. Unlike the bumps, the snags were different sizes. I knew they didn't come with the suit. They came from wear and tear.

The man also wore a brown hat with a brim. Just above the brim, a black ribbon was wrapped around the hat. Except for Chief Dan Mathews in reruns of *Highway Patrol* or Sergeant Joe Friday in reruns of *Dragnet* or Lieutenant Tragg in reruns of *Perry Mason*, I had never seen anyone in real life wear a hat like the one on Joe's head. As far as I knew, only television cops wore them, and they existed in a grainy black-and-white fictional world. Joe didn't look like a cop in any world. He looked mysterious and unapproachable.

I worked up my courage. "Are you Joe?"

The man took a long cigar from his mouth and growled, "Who wants to know?"

I stood as straight as I could and said, "My name is Marcus Plato Hanlon, and I'm looking for a part-time job." As I spoke, the man studied his cigar. The part he kept in his mouth was wet, darker, flatter and more ragged than the other end of his cigar. The lit end had a large ash but no smoke. I suspected the cigar had rested in his mouth for some time.

After about thirty seconds, he mumbled, "I'm Joe Capp. I'm the owner." Then he rattled off a series of questions: "What makes you think you can work for me? What do you need a job for? Why aren't you in school? How old are you, anyway? How much can you lift? Have you ever been in trouble?" He rattled off even more questions as fast as a machine gun pumps out bullets. I found it difficult to take them all in and figure out how to answer him.

I put out my hand to shake his. At first, Mr. Capp ignored my hand. He simply stared at me. Then, he put the cigar back in his mouth, turned toward me, and shook my hand. I made an extra effort to make sure my grip was strong. Then I started to answer his questions. I said I was eighteen years old and a high school student who had never been in any trouble. I also said I would start work at Transamerica as soon as I graduated. Finally, I told him I needed a job and would do any odd jobs to make some money.

In his raspy voice, Mr. Capp asked, "So what do you need the money for, kid?"

I could have told him all kinds of things. Some might have impressed him more, but I decided to tell him the truth. "I want to make enough money to take a girl to the senior prom."

For the first time, Mr. Capp's expression changed. I didn't know what was coming. He burst out laughing and said to the bartender, "Did you hear that, John? The kid wants to take a girl to the prom." Mr. Capp turned away from me. I felt a sense of doom. He didn't look at me when he said, "You can start now. I'll pay you a buck an hour. Your job will be to bring stuff up from the basement for the bar, help the kitchen staff unload deliveries, bus tables when we're short staffed, keep the sidewalk clean out front, and do anything else anyone asks you to do. For today, John will give you your orders. Whatever he says goes, understand?"

"Yes, sir, Mr. Capp. Thank you, Mr. Capp."

He snapped back, "Well, what are you waiting for, kid? Get to work."

During my first afternoon on the job at Capp's Corner, I ran up and down stairs to bring supplies, mostly bottles of liquor. Between runs, I swept the floor inside and the sidewalk outside. The sidewalk straddled two streets. The entrance to the bar was at the corner where the streets met. I was so busy that I didn't have time to examine the sidewalk spots. Time passed quickly. By eight o'clock, I had put in four hours and my legs felt like rubber.

I didn't know how long I was expected to work. Just as that thought crossed my mind, John said, "You can go now." I wasn't sure if he meant I could go permanently or just for the night. As I grabbed my jacket, John said, "See you tomorrow just as soon as you finish school. Let me get your pay." He turned around to the cash register and hit a button with the side of his right hand. The drawer to the cash register opened with a clang. John extracted some money and handed me four one-dollar bills. He laughed as he said, "Don't spend it all in one place, kid."

I carefully tucked the bills into my wallet. I now had twenty percent of the cost of the prom tickets. If I could keep this job for at least five days, I would have the ticket cost covered. If I could keep this job for fifteen days, I would have enough money to buy Mary Ellen a corsage and take her out for dinner after the prom. I knew she would look beautiful. Of course, I was getting ahead of myself. I couldn't even ask Mary Ellen until I had enough money and something to wear. This weekend, my mother and Aunt Edna had promised to take me to buy a suit. My prom prospects looked up.

Thoughts of Mary Ellen, the prom, and my future career turned my legs of rubber into legs of steel. I had new energy. I had purpose. My walk home seemed like nothing. When I walked through our apartment door, I found a note on the kitchen table. It rested against the front of a dinner plate. The plate held my dinner that my mother had prepared before she left for work.

The note was brief. It said, "I couldn't wait for you to get home from school. Here's your dinner."

My mother wrote just like she spoke. She was a woman of few words, no matter which voice took over. Of course, my mother didn't know I now had a part-time job. When I left for school, I didn't know I would have a job, either. I hoped she would be home from work before I had to leave for school in the morning so I could tell her about it. Part of me thought she would be pleased about the job. Another part of me wasn't sure she would be pleased about the reasons for it. She might think a prom was a waste of time and money. I would find out soon enough.

After I ate my meal and completed my homework, I rinsed and washed my dinner plate. Then I wiped down the counter and the kitchen table. I wanted everything to look spic and span when my mother got home from work. Like always, I knew she would be beat. About ten thirty, I went to bed. I expected to fall asleep right away. My body was tired, but my mind was wide awake. My imagination was on overload. I pictured Mary Ellen in her formal dress. I pictured us as we would enter the school gymnasium. I pictured the prom decorations and our surprise at the room's transformation. I pictured our first dance and the smiles on other students' faces as we would move across the dance floor. Those images are as strong for me today as they were then.

Morning came. My dreams were shattered by the clang of my alarm clock. It was six thirty, a half hour earlier than usual. I quickly washed and dressed. I decided to get up early and put on a pot of coffee. I wanted to put on the best possible front when my mother came though the door. It's something I should have done for her all the time.

As I heard the coffee start to perk, I also heard the key in the door. The knob turned and my mother walked in. She stooped as if she had an anvil on her shoulders. It wasn't the weight of the grocery bag; it was the weight of her job and the world. They were heavy. They brought her down.

"Oh, you're already ready for school, and you've made coffee."

I nodded. "Sorry I was late for dinner last night."

"What was going on at school that made you so late?"

"Nothing."

"Nothing?"

It was time for me to come clean. I told her about my part-time job at Capp's Corners in North Beach. "Why now?" she asked. "You start work at Transamerica soon." I explained I needed to earn money so I could go to the prom.

My mother sat down at the table. I grabbed the handle of the coffee pot, pulled a cup off the counter, filled it, and put it front of my mother. She took a sip. Then she took another. After several sips and many minutes, she raised her head and said, "The prom." After a few more minutes, she said, "I never went to a prom." And, after a few minutes more, she said, "Everyone should get to go to a prom at least once." She finished her coffee. As she left the kitchen to go to bed, she murmured, "We'd better get you that suit."

Chapter 20
Fusspots

I liked my job at Capp's. After each school day, I headed to the restaurant. I always had a lot to do. Most days followed the same routine. Even the clientele was the same. It didn't take me long to see that Capp's had a steady flow of regular customers. However, they were all different.

Capp's attracted some real characters. Most sat at the bar and talked to the bartender or whoever was on either side of them. I have no idea what they talked about. But, whatever it was, from time to time, I heard peals of laughter. I will always remember Capp's as a happy place.

Time at work passed quickly. Saturdays, I started work at ten but finished at six instead of eight. Although Capp's was open on Sunday, it was my day off, just as it was my mother's. Within two weeks, I had set aside enough money to buy prom tickets, a corsage for Mary Ellen, and a little toward dinner. Once I was confident I could meet my prom budget, I had to work up the same amount of confidence to ask Mary Ellen to the prom.

Two weeks went by without any mention of a new suit. I started to worry. But when I returned from Mass on Sunday morning, my mother declared, out of the blue, that it was time to buy me a suit. She informed me that we were off to meet Aunt Edna and head to The Emporium. To her, The Emporium represented the best in everything, especially clothes. With all the stores in San Francisco, I'm not sure why my mother chose The Emporium as her source for what she described as good quality clothes.

My mother bought my underwear from J.C. Penney, not The Emporium. She wouldn't buy my underwear from anywhere else. According to her, J.C. Penney's Stafford underwear was the best. I could never figure out what difference it made where we bought underwear. Other than my mother, I didn't know anyone who cared. Except for gym class, it wasn't as if anyone saw what brand I wore. The guys in my class couldn't care less.

For outerwear, my mother held The Emporium in higher esteem than any other department store, including J.C. Penney. Or maybe it just because J.C. Penney had closed its San Francisco store and she wasn't prepared to take public transit to Oakland or San Bruno. It was one thing to order underwear over the telephone; it was another thing to buy a suit. According to my mother, a suit had to be tried on, fitted, and cuffed. It wasn't something we could order from a catalog. By the way she explained the intricacies of a suit, I wondered aloud why we weren't going to a store like Brooks Brothers or a tailor who would custom make one for me. My mother promptly informed me she wasn't made of money. "The Emporium will do just fine."

Of course, Aunt Edna insisted we should just go to a thrift shop where we might be able to get three or four suits for less than the cost of one new one. To her credit, my mother had no interest in a thrift shop today and told Aunt Edna so. Aunt Edna had met her match.

Once we entered The Emporium, we didn't have to go far to find the men's wear department. It was on the first floor. As we walked in, Aunt Edna suggested, "Maybe we should visit the basement first to see if there are any bargains on suits."

My mother ignored her and kept walking toward men's wear. I could see racks of suits in the distance. As we got closer, a white-haired salesman approached us and offered to help. He was dressed in a gray pinstriped suit with a white shirt and a red polka-dotted tie. He looked like someone who might appear in a magazine. My mother told him, with noticeable pride in her voice, that I needed a suit appropriate to wear to work at Transamerica. I had never heard her use that voice before. She sounded more like Grace Kelly than Lauren Bacall. Her pitch was higher and she enunciated every word.

She kept it up as she went to explain that I also needed this suit to attend the senior prom. Inwardly, I chuckled as my mother spoke. She seemed as enamored of this salesman as I was impressed by his attire. For a little while, I saw my mother leave the Tenderloin behind and try to be from somewhere else. I couldn't imagine any of the Nob Hills denizens spoke the way my mother did that morning. I have no idea what part of San Francisco society my mother tried to represent. It was as foreign to me as the sound of her voice.

The salesman, who introduced himself as Mr. Hill, picked up a white cloth tape measure, a small pad of paper, and a pencil. He wrapped the tape around my chest and then across my shoulders. He wrote numbers down on the pad of paper. He then drew the tape from the end of my right shoulder to my right wrist, then the end of my left shoulder to my left wrist, and then around my waist, and wrote those numbers down as well. Lastly, he measured the inside of my legs from the crotch to my ankles. I'm glad he told me in advance, because I would have been startled. After he measured each leg, as he did with all the other numbers, he wrote down them down on the pad of paper.

"What did madam and sir have in mind with respect to suit color?"

To me, he sounded like someone who lived on Nob Hill. I have no idea where he lived. But he didn't sound or look like anyone who lived in the Tenderloin. Today, neither did my mother. "As I said before," my mother replied, "my son will be going to work at an insurance company, so he needs a suit that befits his new job." "Befits" was not a word I had ever heard my mother use before, either. I was in awe. Not only did she use a lofty voice, but now she also used lofty words.

"Perhaps a navy blue or charcoal gray suit," Mr. Hill suggested.

Aunt Edna chimed in with "I like brown."

Mr. Hill frowned. "A gentleman never wears brown in town."

Poor Aunt Edna. Every time she stepped up to bat today, she struck out.

As Aunt Edna stood with her mouth agape, we watched Mr. Hill pull four suits. All four were single breasted. One was, as Mr. Johnstone had suggested, navy blue, and another was charcoal gray wool. The third and fourth suits were surprises. The third was navy with faint squares. He called them "windowpanes." At least that's what I thought he said. The fourth was a lighter gray one, and it had a pattern. He called it "glen check." I can't remember the fabric types. I liked all four suits. However, I must admit the solid navy blue suit appealed to me most. I knew Mr. Johnstone would approve. Before I could say anything, I heard my mother say, "I like the solid navy. I think Marcus should try it on first."

Mr. Hill led me to the changeroom area. There were several doors. He opened one, which revealed a little room with a mirror on one wall and a large hook on another. The room also had a small chair in the corner next to the mirror. Mr. Hill hung the suit on a large hook and left me to try it on. As he closed the door behind him, he said, "The pants will be far too long. Just roll them up when you leave the room. We will alter the pants and jacket to match your measurements." My mother was right: a suit had to be tried on. They had intricacies such as styles, colors, patterns, fabrics, and most importantly, fit.

I took off my shoes, windbreaker, sweater, and jeans. I opened up the suit jacket and found a pair of trousers. It took me a few minutes to figure out how to release the bar to get the pants off the hanger. I pulled the trousers on. Mr. Hill was right—they were way too long. So I did my best to roll them up. The excess fabric almost reached my knees. I put the jacket on. It fit pretty well except, like the pant legs, the sleeves were too long. Now I knew why he wrote all those numbers down on his pad of paper. I put my shoes back on and walked out. Mr. Hill greeted me. "Let's go to the three-way mirror where we can get a better look." I followed him. "Please step up onto to the platform so our tailor will be able to chalk any changes." With all the adjustments this suit needed, the navy blue would become white with chalk after the tailor was through.

My mother and Aunt Edna walked over. Neither said a word. I couldn't tell if they liked me in the suit or not. All of a sudden, I heard Aunt Edna exclaim, "Oh, Marcus! You look so grown up." My mother smiled and nodded her head. When I saw my reflection, I thought I looked like a guy trying to be grown up in a suit made for someone else who was at least a foot taller than I was.

In a matter of minutes, a man in gray pants and waistcoat, white shirt, and tie came up to us. He also wore an off-white cloth tape measure around his neck. On his left wrist, he wore what looked like a lump of cloth above his wristwatch. Upon closer inspection, I saw it was a blue pincushion. "This is the men's department tailor. He will make your suit fit you perfectly." Mr. Hill didn't offer the tailor's name. Later, I heard Mr. Hill call him Sam.

The tailor bent down to adjust the pant length first. He asked me if I wanted the pants hemmed or cuffed. I had no idea and said so. "Well, a well-dressed gentleman's pants should always be cuffed, although some of the younger men favor a plain look."

"Cuffed," I said.

At the same time and in perfect harmony, my mother and Aunt Edna said, "Cuffed."

The tailor took his chalk and marked where the cuffs should be. Then he took pins from his wrist cushion and folded a cuff around each leg. He measured the inseam on each leg and wrote it down on a beige-colored tag. I was impressed by his speed. After both legs were marked and pinned, he stood back to survey his work. "Yes, that will do nicely."

The tailor walked back toward me and put his hands on each of my shoulders. "Your right shoulder slopes a little, but I can tailor your jacket so it will be unnoticeable." I had no idea my right shoulder sloped. Maybe that's why I was such a lousy pitcher. Just as he did with each pant leg, the tailor took his chalk and marked where each sleeve of the jacket should end and folded the arms up inside the sleeves. Then he measured the inseam of each arm and wrote it down on the beige-colored tag. He measured each arm from the nape of my neck to the end of each sleeve. He wrote the measurements on the tag, as well. As before, he stood back to survey his work. "Yes, that will do nicely."

The tailor ran his hand down my back. "I'm not happy with the way the jacket drapes down the center back seam. The center vent should hang together and not separate. I will tailor your jacket to make it hang properly." I didn't know what to make of his observation, but I knew I was being dealt with by a real professional. He should have a name that started with Mister. "Sam" wasn't enough for his kind of talent.

"Turn around now, please, so I can examine the front of the jacket." The tailor fastened and unfastened each of the two buttons on the suit jacket. "You chose wisely. With your build, a two-button jacket is better than a three-button one."

"Why?" I asked.

The tailor explained that a two-button jacket flatters the figure. It makes the wearer look slimmer and taller. Sam knew I needed all the help I could get. "Of course, you know you should only ever fasten the top button. The bottom button always remains open." I wondered why a suit came with a second button if it wasn't used. It remains a mystery to this very day. The men's department proved to be a real education for me.

The lessons I learned from the tailor stuck with me for the rest of my life. As I took off the jacket, the tailor told me my shirt size: a 17½-inch collar and 33-inch sleeves. From then on, whenever I needed a new suit, I asked for this tailor who, I subsequently learned, did have a full name. He was Mr. Samuel Perkins. When he left his employment at The Emporium several years later, I followed him to Kuppenheimer's, and after it went bankrupt, I followed him to Men's Wearhouse. I would have followed Mr. Samuel Perkins to any men's clothing store. I knew he would make sure I looked the best I could, given my size and shape. Mr. Perkins made me feel good about myself in a way Mr. Hill didn't at The Emporium when my mother bought me my first navy blue suit.

My mother and Aunt Edna showed great patience while I was fitted for my suit. The whole process took about an hour and a half. While I changed back into my regular clothes, Mr. Hill rang up the bill. I have no idea how much the suit cost. I came out of the changeroom to see my mother remove many bills from a brown pay packet envelope. It might have taken her entire life savings. Yet she didn't seem at all disturbed. Instead, she seemed proud, not only because she was able to buy my first suit, but also because she was able to invest in my future. As my mother completed the transaction, Mr. Hill said the suit would be ready by the end of next week. She informed him we would stop by next Sunday, at which time I would try on the suit to make sure it was tailored as measured and as promised.

As we turned away from the men's department, my mother said, "I don't know about anyone else, but I'm hungry." This was music to my ears. Aunt Edna suggested we go upstairs to the mezzanine for bay shrimp sandwiches. My mother overruled her. "I want a beer and something more than one of those fancy sandwiches without any crusts. Let's go to Lefty O'Doul's. We can have bay shrimp sandwiches next Sunday when we pick up the suit."

We trotted off to Lefty's, where we lined up to pick out our sandwiches. My mother chose roast beef with gravy and mashed potatoes. Aunt Edna chose sliced turkey on white bread with coleslaw. I chose roast beef on a bun with french fries. My mother ordered a beer, Aunt Edna ordered a black coffee, and I ordered a coke. We took our trays to a corner table and sat. My mother sighed. While I tried to figure out what to make of her expression, she surprised me. "Well, Marcus, now that you have your suit, I believe it's time for you to ask your young lady to the prom." I nearly choked on my sip of coke.

"Prom! Young lady!" exclaimed my Aunt Edna. In between bites of my sandwich, I explained to Aunt Edna I wanted to ask my friend Mary Ellen to the prom. I also told her that I worked at Capp's Corner to earn enough money to buy tickets, a corsage, and dinner after the dance. "Why didn't you say something? I would have helped you pay for it," said Aunt Edna.

Now it was my turn to sigh. "Aunt Edna, a guy can't ask his aunt or his mother to pay for his dates. I would be embarrassed." Now, it was Aunt Edna's turn to sigh. She said nothing. We ate the rest of our lunch in silence.

Chapter 21
Step Aside

Monday morning rolled around, and I left for school. While my classes and shift at Capp's Corner were uneventful, my mind was preoccupied. My mother was right: it was time to ask Mary Ellen to the prom. Now that my suit was almost ready and I had enough money saved for the prom, nothing stood in the way of the prom except I had to ask Mary Ellen to be my date and she had to accept.

While I carted boxes up and down the stairs at Capp's, I resolved to ask Mary Ellen to the prom the next day. I'm not sure why I thought it was such a big deal. Mary Ellen had already given me hints, which I interpreted as encouragement. However, I heard the guys at school and some of the regulars at the bar complain about the fickleness of girls and women. The married bar regulars were even tougher on their wives. I wondered what it was about women that caused these guys so much confusion. I started to have doubts. What if Mary Ellen turned me down after all my efforts to get a part-time job and my mother's investment in a new navy blue suit?

I turned to my sidewalk spots on the way home from work. My spots have always been constants in my life, so I focused on them. As always, they steadied my mind. By the time I reached Hayes Street, I decided to ask Mary Ellen to the prom first thing tomorrow before our classes started. I wasn't going to let my friends, especially Nobby, or the bar regulars put me off. I looked upon the prom as my right of passage from schoolboy to man about town. I was going to show the world I could get a date, look smart, and treat a girl I liked to a lovely evening.

I combed my hair carefully and put on a clean shirt and my best sweater to prepare for the morning's big event. The sun shone. If I had known how to whistle, I would have done so as I walked to school. Long before the first bell rang, I stood at my locker and pulled out the books I needed for the day. Out of the corner of my eye, I spotted Mary Ellen as she walked down the hall to her locker across the hall from mine. I closed and secured my locker. I gave her time to enter her combination on her lock. Once I heard it click open, I walked over.

For some silly reason, I thought of Winston Churchill. I don't know why. I didn't see myself as a warrior. I didn't believe a prom invitation was a battle to be won. Maybe it was because Churchill was roly-poly, like me. Maybe I wanted his courage. Maybe I wanted his eloquence. As I reached Mary Ellen, she smiled. "Hi, Marcus." For some reason and for the very first time, no words came to mind. I had never had any trouble when I spoke to Mary Ellen. Maybe it was a battle after all. I was stunned. "Is everything all right, Marcus?"

I swallowed hard and blurted out in one breath, "Yes, and will you go to the prom with me? I have new suit and I saved money so I can get you a corsage and we can go to dinner and everything."

Now it was Mary Ellen's turn to stand in stunned silence. My mouth was agape. My mind was in a frenzy. Nothing had gone as I had hoped. I had rehearsed how I planned to ask Mary Ellen to the prom at least a thousand times in front of the mirror. But it hadn't gone as planned. Did she think I was from outer space? Would she say yes? Would she say no? Worse, would she think I was crazy? After what seemed an eternity, Mary Ellen rewarded the foolish way I had expressed my invitation with "Yes, Marcus, I would be delighted to accompany you to the prom."

Based on her answer, you might think my mind would instantly quiet and return to its normal rhythms. Instead, it swirled even more. I leaned against the adjoining locker to make sure I didn't fall down. I almost failed to hear her say, "We can talk about it later. See you during lunch period." Mary Ellen swiveled on her right toe and walked away. I was dizzy as I watched her go, and I stayed on cloud nine until I saw her again at lunch. It may not have been a Churchillian moment, but it was my moment. I was as happy as any guy could be.

During lunch, and from then on until prom night, Mary Ellen spoke of nothing but the prom. She wanted to know everything about my new navy blue suit and when I was going to pick it up. She wanted to know what color tie I was going to wear with the suit and if it would complement her dress. She wanted to know how we were going to get to the prom and where we were going to dine after. She wanted to know what type of corsage I planned to buy—wrist or shoulder—and what type of flowers I planned to select for it. She wanted to know when I planned to order the corsage and when I was going to pick it up. I wish I could say I had answers to all of Mary Ellen's questions. I didn't, and I didn't think it mattered.

To me, Mary Ellen's questions were based on an excited stream of consciousness. Even if I had answers, I don't think she cared to hear them. I was glad she was enthusiastic. I hadn't given much thought to her corsage. Now I knew that it, along with everything else about the night, required more attention than I had thought possible.

I took my cue from Mary Ellen and asked about the color of her dress. Who knew that a simple question about color could elicit a fifteen-minute response about a color she called mauve? When she finally drew a breath, I made a mistake and asked what I thought was another simple question: "What color is mauve?"

Normally, Mary Ellen was level-headed. She was always relaxed. However, my simple question caused changes in her face that I had never seen before. Her mouth and eyebrows suddenly twisted into something unrecognizable. Her nostrils flared. She placed her hand on her hips and shouted, "Mauve! You don't know what mauve is?"

I hung my head in shame. Then I shook it slowly from left to right. "I'm sorry, Mary Ellen, but I just want to make sure I get you a perfectly colored corsage to go with your dress."

She relaxed. Her face returned to normal. "Oh, in that case, mauve is like a pale purple. I'll bring you a sample of the fabric so you can take it to the florist." Crisis averted. That was my Churchillian moment.

I started to wonder if the prom was worth all this work. Time would tell. Meanwhile, I would keep my part-time job at Capp's and would look forward to Sunday when I picked up my new suit.

Chapter 22
Sunspot

Sunday came, and my mother and I met Aunt Edna in the foyer of
The Emporium. They were as excited as I was to pick up my new suit.
Today, my mother promised Aunt Edna we could go to the mezzanine
afterward for lunch so she could finally order a bay shrimp sandwich.
We arrived at the men's department shortly after eleven, where we
were greeted once again by Mr. Hill. "Ah, I assume you are here to
pick up your suit?" I thought to myself, what other assumption could
he have in mind? Within a few minutes, Mr. Hill returned with a
navy blue suit that I assumed was mine. "I believe we have completed
all the necessary adjustments and they will be to your satisfaction.
Just to be sure, we ask that you to try it on."

I went into the changeroom and removed my sweater, shoes, and
trousers. This time, I knew how to remove the suit pants from the
hanger, and I slipped them on. I caught a glimpse of myself in the
mirror. I had to admit the pants fit and looked good. I put the jacket
on. Wow. The sleeves were just the right length. Mr. Samuel Perkins
was right—this two-button jacket made me look good. I can't say it
made me look slim, but I sure looked less chubby. I put my shoes back
on and walked out of the changeroom so Mr. Hill, my mother, and
Aunt Edna could take a look.

I could tell by their faces that Mr. Samuel Perkins had outdone
himself. He had tailored my suit to fit me perfectly. His was a super-
human achievement. "Yes," said Mr. Hill, "I believe everything is in
order. What do you think, madam?"

My mother didn't often grin. Today was an exception. Her smile literally went from ear to ear. "I think the suit is perfect."

I went back into the changeroom, took off the suit jacket and pants, and carefully hung them on the hanger. I put my other clothes on. As I was doing so, a sensation came over me that I had never felt before. I felt relaxed. I felt comfortable. I felt tall. I felt confident. I felt as if I might actually go somewhere in life. The sensation didn't last long, but it was one that took me by surprise and I have always remembered. Many times later, I wished I could have relived it.

Maybe that's why they're called "changerooms." Maybe they are more than rooms to change from one set of clothing to another. Maybe they can change your life in other ways, too. I could hardly wait to discuss this possibility with my sidewalk spots.

I handed the suit to Mr. Hill, who rearranged it on the hanger. He placed it in a garment bag, which he zipped and handed to me. A garment bag was another first for me. Mr. Hill bid us goodbye and we headed to the mezzanine for lunch.

Aunt Edna didn't disappoint us—she ordered the bay shrimp sandwich. I can't remember what my mother and I ordered. Whatever we had was insignificant compared to the importance Aunt Edna attached to her bay shrimp sandwich. She waxed on about how nicely they cut the bread and removed the crusts. "The shrimp are simply divine. I'd love to have the recipe for the sauce."

My mother and I ate in silence and nodded at Aunt Edna's pronouncements periodically to give the illusion that we were paying attention. After a while, my mother spoke: "Don't you think Marcus looked handsome in his suit? He will look better than all the other boys when he goes to the prom."

Aunt Edna nodded her head. Then, as only Aunt Edna could, she said, "He looks like he might actually come from upper Nob Hill rather than lower Nob Hill."

Chapter 23
Spot Remover

After lunch, we parted ways. Aunt Edna headed home; her laundry awaited her. My mother and I walked home; my mother's bed awaited her. I hung my new navy blue suit in the closet. I remember clearly what I thought: I would wear my suit for the first time to the prom, which was just a few weeks away. I thought wrong.

Less than two hours later, I heard a knock on our door. Except for Aunt Edna, no one ever visited us. And we had just seen her, so the knock caught me by surprise. Why would she be here now? I answered the door, and before me stood two tall men. One was dressed in a suit, and the other was dressed in a police uniform. In an authoritative voice, the man in the suit asked, "Is this the Hanlon residence?"

"Yes," I replied. I heard my mother stir.

"We're from the San Francisco Police Department," he said. "Is your mother or father home?"

"My mother is home."

As the words left my mouth, my mother walked into the room. "What's going on?"

"Mrs. Hanlon?" asked the tall man in the suit.

"Yes."

"Are you related to Edna Hanlon?"

"Yes, I am. Why?"

"I'm afraid we have bad news. Miss Edna Hanlon was hit by a car today."

Both my mother and I said, "What? Is she hurt?"

"We're afraid your sister died on impact. We don't believe she suffered. We're sorry for your loss. We will need you to identify the body."

This was more than either my mother or I could bear. I started to sob. My mother broke down in tears and fell to her knees. Both men stood in stony silence. With great effort, my mother rose and tried to compose herself. "How could this happen?"

Now the man in uniform spoke. "We believe that as she ran to catch the Powell Street cable car, a taxi passed on the inside lane and struck her."

I couldn't bear to hear any more. I ran into the bathroom and shut the door. It was as if my heart jumped out of my chest and into my throat. The lump was so large that I thought I would choke to death. I couldn't breathe. I sat on the toilet seat and gasped. Then I cried and cried as I had never cried before. After a while, who knows how long, my mother tapped on the door and told me that she was going with the policemen to identify Aunt Edna's body. I wish I could say I offered to accompany her and to show her the support that I am sure she needed, but I didn't. I was too distraught and too immature to be of any comfort to anyone. On some level, I knew my grief was a measure of my love for my Aunt Edna. It was no consolation. Aunt Edna could never be replaced.

By the time my mother returned, it was dark. I was sitting at the kitchen table. "Did you have anything to eat?" my mother asked.

"No, I wasn't hungry." I didn't think I would ever by hungry again. My body ached from despair and my eyes burned from tears.

"We'll have to think about funeral arrangements. Green Street Mortuary handled my parents' funerals. If it was good enough for them, I guess it should be good enough for Edna."

I couldn't get over how matter-of-fact my mother was over the death of her sister. No funeral could ever be good enough for my Aunt Edna. I just couldn't get my head around the idea that she was no longer alive. Thoughts of her funeral and burial were beyond my grasp. Yet my mother was in full organizational mode. She picked up the telephone and called Green Street. She told them where they could pick up Aunt Edna's body. She made an appointment for the next morning to complete funeral and burial details. Her call took no longer than ten minutes. Then she called the bar and told the person who answered that she wouldn't be in until Monday afternoon.

My mother told me that Aunt Edna's visitation would be Thursday evening. Although the car had crushed Aunt Edna's chest, Mother said her face looked good, so her casket would be open during the visitation. The funeral mass would be at Saints Peter and Paul Church on Friday morning, and her interment would follow right after. My mother recited these events as if they were an everyday occurrence. While my world had fallen apart, she had started to put hers back together. At the time, I thought she was being indifferent. Later I reminded myself that my mother loved her sister. As a result, I came to understand how people cope and grieve. They do it in different ways. For the time being, though, the lump in my throat was ever present. The only difference was it varied in size. I was on the verge of tears for many days after Aunt Edna's death. Years later, memories of her still cause a lump in my throat and my eyes to well up with tears.

As I walked to school, I focused on my sidewalk spots. Today, for the first time in a long while, I spoke out loud to them, which seemed to help me manage my sorrow better. I don't know if any passersby reacted; I didn't care. Some guys kicked cans down the road; I spoke to sidewalk spots. This was how I chose to cope and grieve. I couldn't be indifferent to Aunt Edna's death nor to my precious spots. With the focus on my part-time job and the prom, I had ignored them for too long. They were the great constant in my life and source of hope.

When I walked into my homeroom, my teacher said that Mr. Johnstone wanted to see me in his office. Before I could make it out the door, Nobby caught up with me. "Marcus, I am sorry to hear about your Aunt Edna. I know how much she meant to you." I was overwhelmed by Nobby's expression of sympathy. It was a side of him I had never seen. But then again, until now, neither of us had any occasion to experience this kind of anguish. Losses for us had always been in sports.

Mr. Johnstone was solicitous. He said that my mother had called him and explained the circumstances of my aunt's death. He said both he and the school were there to help both me and my mother during this time of sorrow. "Of course, you will be excused from school on Thursday afternoon so you can prepare for your aunt's viewing and all day Friday so you can attend her funeral service and burial." Mr. Johnstone sounded just like my mother. He was matter-of-fact. I thought such evenness must be some kind of grownup attribute I had missed or not yet earned even though, as far as I was concerned, I was already grown up.

Monday, Tuesday, Wednesday, and Thursday mornings droned on. All my classmates, particularly Nobby, Rusty, and Mary Ellen, went out of their way to be kind. Mr. Capp, the other staff, and even many customers did the same. Their kindness didn't seem to make any difference to my state of mind. I found my greatest comfort during my walks. On those walks, I was not alone. My sidewalk spots gave me all the comfort and kindness I needed.

Thursday, after an early dinner, I put on my white long-sleeved dress shirt and my new navy blue trousers. I selected a dark tie from the assortment Mr. Johnstone had given me. It took me several attempts to tie it right. I put on my brown hard-soled Sunday shoes, which were my only dress shoes. Lastly, I put on the jacket to my new navy blue suit. I never dreamed I would wear it to a funeral first, least of all Aunt Edna's. As I did up the top button on the jacket, I wondered how I would feel when I wore this suit to the prom in a few weeks. It didn't matter. The prom was now a low priority compared to what lay before my mother and me tonight and tomorrow.

My mother arranged for a taxi to pick us up and take us to the funeral home. She said the man who organized everything for tonight and Aunt Edna's burial was called a funeral director. She didn't tell me his name, but she did tell me he asked us to arrive about twenty minutes before visitors were due to arrive. He wanted to give us time to be alone with Aunt Edna. I felt that I would need twenty hours, not just twenty minutes, to come to terms with what we were about to do. This was my first funeral, and I really had no idea what to expect, much less how to conduct myself. So far, I had contributed nothing to Aunt Edna's death except tears.

The funeral director took us into what looked like a living room that you might find in a palace. As we came through the entryway, I spotted a small sofa and a coffee table, of all things. At the other end of the room, I saw a big shiny wooden box, which I figured contained Aunt Edna. On another wall, but close to the box, were two chairs unlike any I had ever seen. They had high backs and were covered in a multi-colored patterned fabric. The funeral director suggested we sit in them after we paid our respects to Aunt Edna and while we waited for guests to arrive. He referred to them as upholstered chairs. This was another first. I didn't know the chairs had names like "upholstered."

In front of the casket was a miniature prayer bench. It could hold two people, but I suspected it was made for one. The funeral director led us to Aunt Edna. To my surprise, she looked like she always did. I thought she might sit up and greet us. Weirdly and suddenly, I felt better about why my mother and I were there. I also knew why my mother had sought out a funeral home. Somehow, this place made something tough more bearable.

Aunt Edna's hair was beautifully done. Her makeup looked good, too, but I could tell someone else had put it on. Aunt Edna was always more generous with her rouge and lipstick. Just the same, she looked peaceful, which amazed me since she had suffered such a terrible accident. I had feared her expression might have frozen at the moment of impact. Not so.

My mother asked me if I was okay. I guess she noticed the intensity of my gaze and my silence. "Doesn't she look beautiful, Marcus?"

"Yes," was all I could say. Then, for some bizarre reason, I said, "I wish they had put her sunglasses in one hand and her black patent leather handbag in the other. I wonder where they are."

For a moment, my mother was silent. "Oh, Marcus, her glasses and purse were pretty much destroyed in the accident." Mystery solved.

My mother knelt on the little prayer bench. She made the sign of the cross, and I assume that she prayed for Aunt Edna's soul. It's what I did when it became my turn to kneel on the prayer bench. I also took a little more time to pray for other things. I asked God to help me get through the next twenty-four hours. And, if it wasn't too much, I asked God to keep my mother safe.

After our turns on the prayer bench, we sat in the upholstered chairs. Before long, visitors started to arrive. The first one through the entryway was one of my former "uncles." He had dated Aunt Edna for about two years until they parted company. He was in tears. He wasn't the last of my former "uncles" who came to pay their respects. At least four more came, and all cried. Because they were so distraught and claimed to love her so much, it made me wonder why none had married Aunt Edna. I would never know.

I was surprised and happy when Nobby and Rusty came in. They both called me Marcus and shook my hand. I guess we were growing up, after all. Nobby knelt down on the prayer bench. Rusty didn't. I didn't think any less of him, but for some reason, I thought more of Nobby. Until then, I didn't think prayers formed any part of his life. I learned something new about Nobby. I was not surprised when Mary Ellen also came. She always knew the right thing to do, and it's why I cared for her so much. The same was true for Mr. Johnstone, who also came to pay his respects on behalf of the school.

I was overwhelmed when Mr. Capp, John, Edie, Bev, and others from Capp's Corner came in throughout the evening. As I did with all my friends, I introduced them to my mother. She was gracious and thanked them as she shook their hands. She singled Mr. Capp out for special thanks for his time and for my part-time job.

As Mr. Capp was about to leave, he shook my hand and slipped me a white envelope. "Here, kid. We passed my hat around and took up a little collection for you. Don't worry about coming into work tomorrow and Saturday. This should help you with those prom expenses. By the way, your suit looks good." I didn't know what to say and tried to give the envelope back to him. I explained that I had saved enough for the prom. Mr. Capp replied, "Then buy yourself a new shirt to go with your new suit and maybe a pair of shoes from this decade. The ones you're wearing look like they're prewar. And, maybe, kid, you'll want to get yourself a hat like mine."

For the first time in four days, I smiled. For a moment, his crack about the hat made me forget why we were there. I wondered how he knew I needed another shirt. As for my shoes, I had never thought about them until now. As I stared down and looked at them, I realized they were chunky and maybe unsuitable for dancing. If I stepped on Mary Ellen's toes, I might break them. I put the envelope in my jacket pocket and made a mental note to look for a new shirt and a new pair of shoes.

Aunt Edna's visitation was scheduled for two hours. At one time, a line formed of visitors who wanted to use the prayer bench. All evening, my mother and I greeted people. We never had time to sit on the upholstered chairs again. Aunt Edna was well known. Friends from her church showed up. Like Rusty, they didn't use the little prayer bench. Friends from her work also came by.

One gentleman took my mother aside. I couldn't hear what he said, but I could tell by my mother's facial expression that what he said was important. Later, my mother told me he worked in personnel at Aunt Edna's company. He promised to send papers to us so my mother and I could claim life and accidental death insurance benefits. This was a surprise to us. My mother would receive fifty thousand dollars in death benefits, and I would receive five thousand dollars.

Another gentleman arrived, smartly dressed in a suit. His hands were clasped in front of him and he was holding a hat that matched his suit. After he waited his turn in line to speak with my mother, he introduced himself as Aunt Edna's insurance agent. "I saw her death notice in the *Chronicle* and I wanted to pay my respects and to let you know that Edna had provided for you and your son with life insurance. I will give you my card, and when you are ready, please call me, and I will help you complete the necessary claim forms." I could tell my mother was shocked by his news. On top of the benefits from Aunt Edna's employer, my mother stood to inherit a considerable amount of money as a result of her sister's death. I could tell by my mother's face that she found no joy in these gains. I knew she would give all we had to bring Aunt Edna back. Over the past few days, my mother had lamented over all the times she and her sister had quarreled.

My job was to remind her about all the good times they had, which far exceeded the bad ones. By the time nine o'clock came, we still faced a line of visitors who had come to pay their respects. I was surprised by the support, but I was even more surprised by those who stood in line. Neighbors, who seldom even nodded when we passed by, showed up. People from work, who seldom gave my mother the time of day, showed up. People who were completely unknown to us, and remained unknown, also showed up. Thankfully, the funeral home locked the doors so by nine fifteen, Aunt Edna's visitation was over.

All we had left to do was to attend tomorrow's Mass and burial. As we prepared to leave Green Street Mortuary, the funeral director told us the limousine would pick us up at nine to allow enough time for us to reach Saints Peter and Paul for the Mass. "Limousine!" my mother exclaimed.

"Yes, Mrs. Hanlon, a limousine is part of our service to you."

"Wow," was all I could say.

The next morning, we stood at the curb as the limousine pulled up to take us to the church. We both wore the outfits we had worn the night before, since we had nothing else. I couldn't believe the length of the limousine, and I couldn't wait to get inside. I wasn't disappointed. The seats were just like the ones in the funeral home. They were upholstered, except these had no pattern. They were dark red.

As usual, traffic in downtown San Francisco was thick. My mother and I could have walked to the church faster than it took the limousine to reach Saints Peter and Paul. However, I knew Aunt Edna would get a kick out of us in the back of a limousine. Like us, she couldn't afford these kinds of luxuries. Unlike us, she had always dreamed that she could one day. The irony was not lost on me.

We didn't know the priest who conducted the funeral Mass for Aunt Edna. It was obvious the priest didn't know her, either. His remarks about her were trite and they fell flat. I ignored them and focused on the service. Mercifully, it was short and few had to endure it. Unlike last night's visitation, attendance at the Mass was sparse.

Aunt Edna had no official pallbearers. Once the service was over, the funeral director and his assistants, all smartly dressed in gray pinstriped suits, wheeled her casket through the front doors of the church and hoisted her casket into the funeral home station wagon. Actually, a "station wagon" is a poor word to describe it. I was certain it was called something official, but if so, I had no idea what the official word was. After the casket was loaded, the funeral assistants and the priest got into the station wagon, too. The funeral director opened the back door of the limousine so my mother and I could enter. He then drove, and we began our journey to a place my mother called Colma, where she said that San Franciscans bury their dead.

Our limousine followed the station wagon. The drive took about forty-five minutes. My mother and I exchanged no words until we reached Colma. I couldn't believe what I saw and what I didn't see. Instead of houses, I saw graves, more graves, and even more graves. My mother must have noticed my change in demeanor. "Is there something wrong?" Just as it was difficult to take in the scene, it was difficult for me to find the words to ask my mother about all the graves. "Marcus, Colma has more dead people than live ones. San Francisco has some cemeteries, but they're full. So everybody else gets buried here."

"Oh," was all I could say. As we came to a stop behind the station wagon, I wondered what kids did here. Where would a guy like me play or find any sidewalk spots?

The burial was shorter than the funeral Mass. The priest did his duty. If possible, he was more perfunctory. My mother took a handful of dirt from around the grave and tossed it onto Aunt Edna's casket, which now nestled deep in the hole. I followed suit. Then we followed the funeral director back to the limousine, which returned us to the curb where we had started the day. It was just after twelve.

My mother suggested we go out for lunch at a little diner on Hayes Street. After we ordered our lunch, my mother said, "Well, I am glad it's all over. I hope Edna would approve. I did as well as I could for her." She paused. "I wish the priest had known her. Edna deserved to be honored better. His eulogy was pitiful." I nodded. Today we thought alike. We ate our lunch in silence.

Over the next few weeks, my mother and I cleaned out Aunt Edna's apartment. Her place was much bigger than ours. Now that my mother expected an inheritance, I had hoped she might move us into it. Not so. "You can do whatever you want with your share, but I'm saving mine for my retirement." I couldn't argue with her. She made sense. I decided to do the same, except I did spend the money in the white envelope from Mr. Capp.

In the envelope, I found enough money to buy two new white dress shirts and my first pair of black shoes. I bought the shirts in Chinatown. They were cheaper there than at The Emporium. I asked Mr. Johnstone where I should buy a new pair of shoes and what type I should buy. He suggested I go to a Florsheim Shoe Company store and buy a pair of black loafers. I followed his advice. I was hopeful that Mary Ellen's toes would be safe on prom night.

Chapter 24
High Spots

The days between Aunt Edna's death and her funeral seemed to last forever. The days after her funeral seemed to fly by. My part-time job gave me enough money to treat both Mary Ellen and me to the prom. The night exceeded my expectations. Mary Ellen said she had the time of her life. I hoped the night exceeded her expectations, too.

Graduation day came and went. My mother told me how proud she was of me. Before Mary Ellen started her four years at Santa Clara University, she departed San Francisco for Oregon to spend the summer with her grandparents. Before starting his full-time career in the army, Rusty left for basic training at Fort Ord. Before he continued his career, which could only be described as questionable, Nobby started to carry a briefcase, which was handcuffed to his wrist. The day after school ended, I started my new job and classes at night school. My life was good. My sidewalk spots fascinated me more.

If I thought my workplace would be different from high school, I was mistaken. At work, we sat at desks. They were arranged in rows just like high school. The only difference was my insurance company desk was bigger and had drawers on both sides. Our workplace even had lockers like high school.

I started my insurance career in the claims department. I was assigned a desk next to a girl who started the same day I did. Her name was Harper Carlson. Like me, she was a recent high school graduate. Unlike me, she wasn't a part-time college student. Our job, along with eight other women, was to assess dental claims. We either approved or declined them. I discovered that I began where I could do the least financial damage if I made a mistake. Dental claim amounts were low, so the risk was low. If I did well with dental claims, I could advance to medical claims, which posed more financial responsibility. If I did well with medical claims, I could advance to disability and life insurance claims, which posed even greater financial responsibility. Sometimes, millions of dollars were involved. For now, I was concerned with dental claim policies and procedures to make sure I authorized payments properly. Because nighttime meant college classes, I was happy my daytime job meant less potential for me to do any financial damage to the company.

After a few weeks on the job, Harper said, "Well, Fast Track Jack, how is college? Do you think you'll stick it out?"

I thought when I left high school, I would leave nicknames behind. I was wrong. Nonetheless, I smiled as I tried to make light of her comments and asked, "Why do you call me Fast Track Jack?"

Harper said that it was obvious the company believed I had a future beyond this department. "After all, we were both assigned the same type of work, but the company offered to send you to college. They didn't make that offer to me." Harper also remarked that supervisors and managers spoke to me differently than they spoke to her and the other women in our area.

Her comments stuck in my mind. The last thing I wanted was to be thought of differently. I wanted to fit in and do a good job. I decided to keep my head down and focus on my work. Over time, Harper and I developed a rapport. Although she continued to call me Fast Track Jack, I knew she meant no malice.

A few months went by. One Friday morning, our supervisor called Harper and me to her desk. By the look on Harper's face, I could tell she was worried. I was, too. But we need not have worried. We learned we were both promoted to medical claims. For the next few years, Harper and I followed the same career path. Others followed us, too. Insurance companies promoted from within. If we stayed long enough, we moved up through the ranks.

Harper and I continued to sit next to each other. From time to time, we went out to lunch and she would tell me all about her latest boyfriend, her latest shopping adventure, or her latest exploits with girlfriends. We became friends and stayed friends even after our futures took different paths.

One day, Harper told me that her latest boyfriend had asked her to marry him, and she had accepted. After the wedding, which I attended, she continued to work. She and her new husband came to my graduation from Golden Gate University. Two years later, Harper told me she was pregnant and planned to leave the company to be a full-time mother. I tried to persuade her to come back after the birth of her baby, but to no avail. Just before her baby was due, she left the company for good. I missed her. Harper had been at my side from the beginning of my insurance career.

I moved on from the claims department to a new area in which I would assess applications for insurance as an underwriter. Fortunately, this new department was on the same floor as claims, so I was able to stay in touch with my former colleagues during breaks. While I preferred the faster pace of work as a claims processor over that of an underwriter, I appreciated that this new position required different analytical skills and represented advancement. Over the next thirty years, like many others who also committed their lives to the company, I was moved from one department to another. Each move usually meant a raise and sometimes a promotion. I was grateful for the opportunities the company offered me.

Although she seldom expressed herself, my mother told me how proud she was of my accomplishments after each promotion. As I earned more money, I tried to convince her to accept help from me so she could move into a better apartment. I had moved closer to work as soon as I could afford my own place in North Beach. I wanted her to live nearby and give up her job.

She wouldn't hear of it. Yet I knew that if she didn't make some changes, her body wasn't going to withstand the rigors of the bar forever. She showed many signs of someone who has lost stamina. She rubbed her knees while she sat, and she struggled and groaned when she stood up from a chair. It took her a few minutes before she could stand straight. I worried about her. I should have worried more.

One Friday night, just after I had put on my pajamas and turned down my bed, the telephone rang. I wondered who would call that late at night. I suspected a wrong number as I trundled out of the bedroom to answer it. An unknown voice at the other end said, "Your mother fell and couldn't get up. We called an ambulance, and she's been taken to Saint Francis." Before I could ask any questions, the caller hung up. I ran into the bedroom and put my slacks and shirt back on. As I struggled with my socks and shoes, I wondered what had caused my mother to fall. Why couldn't she get up?

In a big city like San Francisco, you might think it would be easy to find a taxicab. Just as they say that there's never a cop when you need one, there's never a cab when you need one, either, especially at a time of night when people are leaving shows and restaurants. After what seemed to be an hour, I finally hailed a cab. The driver hurried me to the emergency department at Saint Francis Memorial Hospital. I paid him, ran through the emergency room's double doors, and approached the first desk I saw. A woman asked if she could help me. I explained my mother had been brought to the hospital and gave the woman her name. "Yes, Mrs. Hanlon arrived about an hour ago by ambulance. The doctors are with her now. I will let them know you are here. What is your name?" Once I heard that an ambulance had brought my mother to the hospital, I knew her condition was serious. My mother would never give up control to anyone unless she wasn't in control.

The woman told me to take a seat in the area to her left. I couldn't get over the number of people already there. Some were there to be treated, and others, like me, were there to learn about patients dear to them. Saint Francis was a busy place on Friday night. Chairs were soon in short supply. It wasn't too long before none were left. New visitors had to stand.

I waited and waited for a doctor to come out and tell me what was wrong with my mother. Most of the time, I had my head in my hands while I tried to figure out what caused her to fall. Finally, a man in a white coat came out and asked for Mr. Hanlon. He introduced himself as Dr. Young. He explained that he, as an emergency room physician, had examined my mother first. Based on his preliminary diagnosis, he had called in a cardiologist. They concurred that my mother had a stroke. In their opinion, it was unlikely she would make it through the night. "I will take you to see her now. You will find that she's unresponsive."

No sooner than I reached my mother's bedside and held her hand that she took her last breath. It was almost as if she had waited for me to show up.

This time, it was my turn to go to Green Street Mortuary and make the arrangements. I remembered how my mother had said if it was good enough for her parents, it was good enough for Aunt Edna. I knew it would be good enough for her, too. I wasn't disappointed.

I had one night of visitation for my mother followed by a funeral Mass at Saints Peter and Paul and burial in Colma. I didn't cry the way I did when Aunt Edna died. I guess it was because I was older and wiser, and I already had one funeral under my belt. I did cry the night my mother died, but just once. I steeled myself for the days of visitation and burial. The lump in my throat felt smaller than before. Maybe it was because my throat was bigger. I had no idea.

The visitation took place Tuesday night from seven until nine. My colleagues from work came to pay their respects. Harper came, too. She came alone and explained that, although her husband wanted to come, he had to stay home to babysit. They now had three children, two girls and a boy. "Guess what?" she asked. I had no idea. "Our son's first name is John after his father and grandfather, and his middle name is Marcus after you." All of a sudden a little lump in my throat became a giant one. I was overcome, but I managed to keep my composure. I hugged Harper harder than I had ever hugged anyone before. She hugged me back with equal force. I was glad she liked the name Marcus. She could have called her son Fast Track Jack.

A few people I didn't recognize also showed up for the visitation. They told me they worked with my mother. I had never met them before, nor had I ever heard my mother mention their names. Just the same, I was grateful they took time to come. I thanked each one as I shook their hands.

I was surprised to see a familiar face. It was Nobby. He came over and hugged me as he whispered, "Playdough, I'm so sorry for your loss."

As soon as he said my nickname, I was brought back to a life I had left many years ago. "Do I call you Nobby, or do I call you Arthur now? And where's your briefcase?"

"Most people call me Mr. Lefkowitz, but you can still call me Nobby." He told me other guys carried briefcases for him now. I wasn't sure what he meant, but I had to admit he looked successful.

Nobby wore a grey pinstriped tailored suit. It must have cost him twice as much as what I paid for my suits. The French cuffs on his starched white shirt revealed jewelry any woman would envy. His tie looked to be red paisley silk. It was tied with a Windsor knot. I'm sure I could have seen my face in the shine on his black wing-tipped shoes. He was still skinny.

Nobby asked, "Has any of the old gang showed up tonight?' By "the gang," I assumed he meant Rusty and Mary Ellen. I shook my head and explained that I had lost touch with both of them after high school. "Too bad. You know we're having a thirty-fifth class reunion in a few weeks. Maybe they'll show up then. It'll be fun. I'm on the committee. I'll tell them you'll be there. What's your address and phone number so we can send you all the stuff?"

I wasn't sure I wanted to face my former classmates so soon after my mother's death, but Nobby was persuasive. I wrote down my home address and telephone number on the back of one of my business cards and handed it to him. Before putting it his pocket, Nobby studied it. "It looks like you've done well, Mister Vice President Playdough."

Within a few days, a package arrived with all the information about the reunion. I decided to go. I filled out the form and sent it in along with my check for fifty dollars. It amused me to pay so much to eat in the cafeteria we had despised as students. I hoped the committee contracted with an outside caterer. Otherwise, I imagined a meal of instant mashed potatoes, mixed vegetables, and mystery meat smothered in gravy. But it didn't matter what was served as long as Rusty and Mary Ellen showed up. I wanted to see them again. What had they been doing for the last thirty-five years?

Chapter 25
Sidelined

Although I planned to attend the reunion, my employer had other plans for me. Together with another company officer, I was asked to assess the possible acquisition of a financial services company that needed a cash infusion from us to survive. We flew from San Francisco to Seattle on Wednesday. I thought we might make it back in time, but our meetings and subsequent analysis took us through to Sunday. As a result, I missed the reunion. Even though I was disappointed, I was happy for the chance to visit another city. During our walks to and from the hotel, I was able to check out Seattle's sidewalk spots. To me, they looked similar to San Francisco's, but I didn't have enough time to develop an affinity with them. If the acquisition became a reality, I hoped my company would send me back to help make the transition. Then I could get to know these spots better.

While we were gone, our own company experienced a major change. We came back to learn we had been acquired by a European financial services company. Our new owner had new ideas for our company. Unfortunately for me, the Seattle acquisition was off. As it turned out, my company also had concerns about its business lines. Our new owners decided to shift our focus toward financial services and away from traditional insurance products. We were top heavy with insurance. As a result, senior insurance management, which included me, was offered financial incentives to leave.

For the time being, incentive packages were optional. I had heard of these plans called "golden parachutes." Those who were over fifty-five called them early retirement packages. Those like me, who were under fifty-five, called them escape hatches. It didn't really matter to me what they were called; I got the message. It was time for me to think differently about my future. I could leave my job now with a financial safety net, or I could stay and look forward to an uncertain future. I decided to escape, though I had no idea what I was going to do next. I knew I wanted to be my own boss. I also knew I wanted to try something different. I wanted to be in a position to assess my own business and put my on own stamp on it.

I met with a headhunter about some insurance job possibilities in San Francisco, but I wasn't optimistic about any of them. Competition for these positions was stiff. Besides, they were still insurance jobs, and I wanted to try something different. I also met with a couple of friends who specialized in real estate. One of them came up with an opportunity to own a business and a house in a small town. The business was a liquor store. The house was a two-bedroom bungalow about a half mile from the store. The town was about one hundred miles from San Francisco. The cost was within my budget.

Like my mother, I had saved the money from Aunt Edna. Thanks to compound interest, it had grown into a sizeable amount. My mother had also left me an inheritance, including the money from Aunt Edna and proceeds from her own life insurance policies. All in all, I had a nice nest egg that would allow me to purchase both the liquor store and the house with no mortgage. My so called "golden parachute" from the company amounted to an annuity that paid me monthly benefits. Although it wasn't enough to live on in a city like San Francisco, it was enough to make do in a city a hundred miles away.

I made several trips to meet the owner of the business and house. His name was Phil, and he impressed me. The name of his store was Phil's Liquor Store. The town was small but seemed active. His business wasn't worth millions of dollars, but it produced a steady income. The owner had a few part-time employees, and he assured me they would stay. The thought of my own store appealed to me. The thought of no suit and tie appealed to me more. I agonized about life in a small town rather than a big city, but once I found sidewalk spots in front of the liquor store and saw all the businesses around it, I took them as prophetic signs. I became convinced this opportunity was meant for me. Through my real estate agent, I made a cash offer, and Phil accepted it. Within three months of my departure from a 35 year career in insurance, I was now the owner of a liquor store and a two-bedroom bungalow.

My friends and colleagues were surprised by my decision. Nonetheless, they congratulated me. More than one asked me if they could buy their booze at a discount. Others joked that I was "spirited" away. I went to bid farewell to Sam Perkins at Men's Wearhouse and told him all about my new venture. I knew he was sorry to see me leave, not just because he was sorry to lose a customer, but also because we had formed a relationship over the years. I assured him that I would be back to San Francisco from time to time and would stop in to visit. "What to you plan to wear to work in your new position?" I hadn't given it any thought, except I knew it wouldn't be a suit and tie.

Sam reminded me that his store carried sportswear, too. Before I left, he sold me three pairs of slacks and some shirts. He also reminded me I would now be on my feet most of the day, so he fitted me for two new pairs of shoes—black and brown. They were like the ones he wore, made by Rockport. The days of high-top Converse canvas, hard-soled shoes, and Florsheim loafers were over.

As I packed up my apartment, I was surprised to hear the telephone ring—I thought it had already been disconnected. It was Nobby, who wondered where I had been. I wondered why he called now. Months had passed since our thirty-fifth high school reunion. Nobby said he had tried to reach me on my business phone, but he was informed that I no longer worked for the company. When he didn't see me at the reunion and couldn't connect with me at my company, he started to worry. Apparently, it took him that long to find my home telephone number on the back of my business card.

I asked Nobby about the reunion. Who had I missed? He told me they had a big crowd, but neither Mary Ellen nor Rusty had shown up. So, as it turned out, I hadn't missed much. We discussed our thirty-fifth reunion for a few minutes more. Nobby reminded me that the class planned another reunion, our fortieth. He hoped I would attend. Then he said, "Marcus, if you needed a job, why didn't you come and see me? I would have put you on my payroll."

Now was my time to ask him a question. It had been on my mind ever since I could remember. "What exactly is that you do?"

Nobby laughed. "I like to call myself a publisher." The thought that Nobby had anything to do with books made me laugh, and I told him so. It made him laugh, too. "Well," he said, "it's a nice way for me to say I make book." Now we both laughed. "I've been doing it since high school, and I've made piles of dough." I always suspected Nobby took bets. Now I knew for certain. I wasn't surprised to learn he made his money this way, but I was surprised by his candor. I told him it was now my turn to worry about him. "Don't bother. I know how to take care of myself."

Nobby then asked, "By the way, what's your new business and where is it?"

"It's a liquor store in the city of Gnome. I bought from a man named Phil, who owned it for almost fifty years."

"What's the name of it?"

"Phil's Liquor Store."

Nobby chuckled. "That's real original. You gotta change the name. Why don't you call it Playdough's Pints? I can't imagine people in a small town buying anything larger."

I wasn't really up for Nobby's sarcasm or his attempts at humor at the expense of my new business. So I just gave him my new address and asked him to put me on the reunion mailing list. I didn't ask him to stay in touch. It was time to leave him and San Francisco behind.

Chapter 26
Cakewalk

As I crossed the Oakland Bay Bridge, the only city in which I had ever lived filled my rear-view mirror. A few friends referred to my move as an adventure. If only it were that.

Lewis and Clark went on an adventure. They took off to explore the unknown west of the Mississippi River without a map. I knew where I was going and what I was going to do, and I had a map. Still, I knew all my experiences from this point forward would be new ones.

My prospects both excited and daunted me. Would customers still patronize the store under new ownership? Would I be successful? Would I like my new house? Would I make friends? Would I like Gnome? What if this new venture didn't work out? What would I do? I mulled these questions over in my mind as I made the trip. At the seventy-mile mark, I realized these questions just caused self-doubt and made me anxious. It was time to set them aside. I focused on this new opportunity and the promise it held for me.

I reached Gnome by noon and went to the liquor store first. Phil was there to greet me along with his three part-time employees. Although they were not scheduled to work, all three of them wanted to welcome me. I was touched by their thoughtfulness. Their gesture removed my doubts. At Phil's suggestion, I gave them some background about my past life. However, I kept my comments brief. I focused on them and how excited I was about the chance to get to know and work with them, the business, and the city of Gnome. They seemed receptive.

Over the next few months, I focused on my business and on the other businesses around me. In particular, I focused on the restaurant that

I depended on for my meals. My culinary skills were limited. While San Francisco offered more restaurant choices, the reality was I dined in just a few places. So, while Gnome offered fewer restaurant choices, it didn't matter. I became a regular diner in a matter of days and acquainted with other regulars in a matter of weeks.

Phil taught me to be careful. He reminded me that in small towns and cities, everyone knows everyone, and most everyone is related. As a result, Phil told me it was important to keep thoughts about people to myself. Any off-hand comments about customers or other diners would be shared. "Remember how we were warned in World War II that 'loose lips sink ships'?" I didn't remember, but I was grateful for his advice, and I took pains to heed it.

Along with his suggestions about how to run the business and get along with others, Phil also suggested I join the Chamber of Commerce as a way to meet local business people and a service club to meet people outside of business. While the people with whom I worked in San Francisco joined clubs, the thought never appealed to me. I couldn't see the benefit of a club membership. Apparently, Gnome was different. Thanks to Phil, I joined the Gnome Chamber of Commerce.

At least a half dozen service clubs operated in Gnome. I had heard of a couple such as Rotary and Lions. However, Phil thought I should accompany him to Kiwanis. I did and was impressed by the welcome I received from its members. I assumed the welcome had more to do with the regard they held for Phil than for me as a prospective member. Just the same, their enthusiasm for the club and its activities made me want to join. I completed the membership form during my first visit and wrote a check for one year's dues. I started to feel that I fit in. Those pesky doubts I had during my drive from San Francisco to Gnome finally evaporated.

After six months, Phil had fulfilled his obligations to me as part of the business sale. He was ready to retire, and I was ready to take the helm. He made it easy for us both. Phil had been a good teacher on all fronts, and he gave me confidence. My employees seemed to like me, too. My comfort level grew as months went by. Before long, I celebrated my first anniversary as the owner of Phil's Liquor Store, and then my second, third, and fourth years. As I was coming up on my fifth anniversary, I wanted to take my employees out for dinner to celebrate.

While I usually treated my staff to a Christmas party and gave them annual bonuses, the anniversary party was special. I asked them to pick the place, although I hoped they would choose somewhere I liked, too.

Because I had spent so much time in San Francisco's North Beach, I had grown to enjoy Italian food, especially pizza. Although I spent a lot of time near San Francisco's China Town, I never developed a taste for Chinese food. Dead ducks in windows put me off. I wasn't a fan of other foreign foods either, such as Mexican. I liked what other people called "comfort food." To me, nothing was more delicious than a bowl of tomato soup and a grilled cheese sandwich. A steak and baked potato were special treats. If I felt adventurous, I ordered a side salad with creamy ranch dressing and poured A1 sauce on my steak. Usually, though, I liked my food plain. I didn't care for spices or garnishes, such as sprigs of parsley. What was the point? And, who eats parsley, anyway?

My employees made me happy with their restaurant choice. It was one I frequented at least three times a week. I should have known it would come down to a choice between two restaurants. Gnome had lots of lunchtime restaurants, but it didn't have many choices for dinnertime. I'm not sure why, except maybe people preferred to be home with their families for dinner.

For our fifth anniversary business dinner, my employees reserved a table for us at the Silver Spoon Steakhouse. I have no idea who came up with the name of this place, and I didn't ask anyone, either. I was afraid such a question might give offense. As many times as I ate there, at no time did I ever see a silver spoon or any other piece of cutlery made of silver. Stainless Steel Spoon Steakhouse would have been a better name for it.

A few days before the anniversary dinner, Nobby called. This was the first time I had heard from him in five years. "How's it going? Have you drunk all your profits?"

I chose to ignore Nobby's attempts at humor and said, "Great."

"Did you receive the information about the fortieth class reunion? Can we count on you this time?" I told him I had not yet made up my mind. Nobby said, "At least twenty classmates have already registered."

"Like who?"

"Well, for starters, Rusty and Mary Ellen signed up and sent in their checks." Nobby rattled off the names of some other classmates, but the moment I heard the names Rusty and Mary Ellen, I knew I would be there, too.

However, I was noncommittal. After Nobby's cracks about my business, I didn't I want to give him the satisfaction of an answer. Instead, I told him I would think about it.

As soon as I got off the telephone, I pulled the reunion information out of the envelope, completed the application, wrote a check, and filled out a return envelope. I placed the form and check inside the envelope and sealed and stamped it. Then I went out the door and mailed it. It took me less than five minutes. Then, I phoned the Mark Hopkins Hotel and made a reservation for three nights. I planned to go to San Francisco a day before the reunion and stay one or two days after. I had a lot to look forward to—an anniversary dinner, almost four days in San Francisco, a class reunion, and finally my chance to stay at the top of the hill instead of the bottom.

The fifth anniversary dinner was fun. My employees surprised me with a cake from our local bakery. Each also gave me a card. I was touched and told them so. They took turns to speak about the last five years. Their comments interested me. They thought they would lose their jobs when I arrived. Instead, they said, I made them feel part of a team. They liked how I treated them differently than Phil did. Although they also liked the previous owner, Phil always made them feel like workers, not partners.

At that moment, I realized why the store was showing greater profits than Phil had led me to expect. He said the store usually generated a ten-percent growth each year, which is what happened my first year. However, during my second and subsequent years, I saw profits grow from fourteen percent to over twenty-two percent. I wish I could say that my management style had been deliberate, but it wasn't. Instead, I relied on two principles. First, I decided to treat my employees the way in which I would want to be treated. Second, I decided I didn't want any adverse publicity that might come about if I let any of my employees go.

My three part-time employees were related to just about everyone in town. If I had to attach weight to either of my management principles, I would have to say the second one was at the forefront of any style I had put into place. It didn't matter how much I liked my employees or how much they may have liked me; I knew that blood is always thicker than water. No matter how long I lived in Gnome, I knew I would always be a newcomer and I would always be "water," no matter how much I paid my employees or how much I contributed to the community.

As we finished our cake and coffee, Margie, who was my oldest employee, spoke. "Marcus, do you mind if I ask you a question?"

"Of course not," I replied. "What would you like to know?"

"Why do you always look down when you walk?"

I wondered if tonight might be a good time to test the waters about my sidewalk spots. While I tried to come up with how I would describe my love of them, Sandra, who was my youngest employee, spoke. "I tell people it's because you're shy."

I didn't know what to say. If Sandra had exchanged comments with "people," it was apparent my behavior had been noticed by others. I knew I looked down more than straight ahead. However, I didn't know if they would understand why I looked down. Would they understand my fascination with sidewalk spots? In response to Margie, I asked, "Don't sidewalks interest you?" The looks on their faces told me all I needed to know. If I told them about my relationship with sidewalk spots, they would think I was odd or worse. Instead, I regrouped, smiled, and said, "Sandra, you are perceptive. I guess I am kind of shy. I'll try to look up more."

Margie, Sandra, and the only male employee of my staff, Tony, laughed. "It's okay, Marcus," Margie said. "We just want to get to know you better and let you know we care. You don't have to be shy with us. We're your friends." I took in what Margie and Sandra had said. I tried to appreciate their sentiments, Perhaps it would be a good idea to look up more and down less.

Tony weighed in: "All my friends think you're a weirdo. I don't, but they do." I was shocked. His comments came out of nowhere, and they threw me off completely. They changed the dynamic of our anniversary party for me and altered my frame of mind. In an instant, I discovered no one really knew me. I resolved that no one had any need to get to know me any better. And my relationship with my sidewalk spots was mine and mine alone. I would keep them to myself. My sidewalk spots would remain off limits to anyone, including my employees.

Chapter 27
Bald Spots

It was sunny when I left Gnome for San Francisco. Despite the lousy outcome of my anniversary dinner, my spirits were raised by the thoughts of a few days off and my fortieth class reunion. It had been a while since I spent any time in San Francisco. Occasionally, I made day trips to attend the odd retirement lunch or funeral for former colleagues, but I never had a reason to stay overnight until this reunion.

My first stop on the way to the hotel was Men's Wearhouse. I wanted to see Sam Perkins, but he wasn't there. The salesman who greeted me said Sam had retired three years ago after the loss of his wife. He thought Sam had moved to Oregon to live with his daughter and her family. I was sad about Sam's misfortune and sadder I could not pay my respects to him over the loss of his wife.

After I left Men's Wearhouse, I decided to drive around my old neighborhood. The Tenderloin didn't look any different; it was just as I remembered it. I wasn't sure that was a good thing. I had hoped it would look better. After I left the Tenderloin, I headed for North Beach. It was just as I remembered it, too, which was a good thing. I didn't think it could be any better. I then left North Beach and headed for the Mark Hopkins Hotel, where I planned to kick off my mini-vacation.

I drove up California Street until I reached two square pillars, each of which bore large lights. They looked like giant heads on top of cement shoulders and marked the entrance for the Mark Hopkins. The hotel sat diagonally on the block, which to me, made the approach to the three canopied front doors look grander than the other hotels nearby.

The doorman approached as I stopped my car. "Yes, sir, will you be staying at the hotel?" I nodded. "Would you like me to take care of your car?" I nodded and handed him my keys. "Do you have baggage, sir?" I nodded. He took my keys and went to the back of my car, where he unlocked the trunk and removed my suitcase. He placed it on a brass rolling luggage cart. "Sir, if you will, please follow me." I nodded.

I didn't know why I couldn't speak. On some level, I thought my words might cause the doorman to think I didn't belong. Yet I knew I could afford to stay, so why shouldn't I speak? I had as much right as anyone to be a guest of the hotel. After all, I owned my own business, I owned my own house, and I had money in the bank. Perhaps I was intimidated by the opulence of Nob Hill. While these thoughts ran through my mind, I also reveled in thoughts about my Aunt Edna and my mother. Aunt Edna would be overjoyed to know I was now able to stay at the top of the hill. My mother, on the other hand, would be concerned that I was about to stay in a place above my station in life.

As the front door of the hotel was opened for me, I set my shoulders straight and decided to enjoy the next few days as a Nob. As I checked in at the reception desk, it was Mr. Hanlon this and Mr. Hanlon that. I had never heard Mr. Hanlon uttered so often in such a short time. I started to feel like a real Nob. No one called me Mr. Hanlon in Gnome; most everyone called me Marcus. As it turns out, some called me weirdo.

The bellboy showed me to my room on the tenth floor. It was larger than any room in which I had ever slept. The bellman pulled out a wooden folding rack. He snapped it open and placed my suitcase on top of it. "Will there by anything else, Mr. Hanlon?" I found my voice and a tip while I informed him everything was fine. It was fine. It was better than fine. Perhaps, I thought, I should skip the reunion and luxuriate in the bed, order room service, and watch television for the next three days.

After I unpacked, I decided to take a shower. The bathroom was almost as big as the apartment my mother and I shared in the Tenderloin. The shower stall was huge. I didn't have to lift my leg over the edge of the two-foot-high bathtub to get in. I walked in. It took me a few minutes to figure out how to turn the shower on and another few minutes to figure out how to adjust the temperature. Once I did, I took the longest shower I had ever taken in my life. I crossed my arms over my chest and let the water fall all over me. I wondered if all the Nobs on Nob Hill lived this way.

After I toweled off and brushed my teeth for the second time that day, I decided against another shave. After I dressed, I planned to walk around North Beach for the rest of the afternoon, revisit sights, and check out my sidewalk spots. Would my spots remember me? I knew I would remember them. After all, I had spent most of my life focused on them. Later, I planned to go to Capp's Corner for dinner. I wondered who brought up the boxes from the basement and swept the sidewalk now.

Rather than walk down California Street, I decided to take a taxi to North Beach. As I walked from the lobby toward the doors, the doorman held one open for me. "Will you need a taxi, sir?" I nodded. Within seconds, I heard his whistle. Within minutes, a taxi pulled up. The doorman opened the back door on the passenger side so I could get in. I handed him a tip. "Where shall I tell the driver to take you, sir?"

"Washington Square," was all I said. The taxi driver asked where I wanted to be let off in Washington Square. "In front of Saints Peter and Paul Church will be fine."

My mother's funeral Mass was the last time I had entered Saints Peter and Paul. When I worked in San Francisco, I had walked by it thousands of times, but I had never gone back in. Today, I went in, said prayers, and lit candles for my mother and Aunt Edna. Even though I thought of them often, those thoughts did not last long. It felt good to pay my respects in a deliberate way. I made a vow to visit Saints Peter and Paul every return visit to San Francisco.

As I left the church, I started to search for my sidewalk spots. In some areas, it was difficult to find them. They had been overtaken by more spots and some larger ones. A part of me wished I had been here to see the birth of the new ones and growth of the old ones. I was devastated to find a section of sidewalk had been replaced. As a result of new sidewalk construction, some of my favorite spots had disappeared. If I had known, I would have said prayers and lit candles for them, too. My discomfort was allayed when I discovered most of the restaurants and other places of business and their sidewalks were where I left them.

It took me about three hours to cover all my sidewalks in Washington Square. By this time, I was hungry. I headed to Capp's, where a hostess greeted me and told me her name was Margot. A hostess was a new addition to Capp's. Joe was nowhere to be seen. I didn't recognize the bartender or any of the wait staff. While five years did not seem to be a long time in the course of my life, it was a long time in this restaurant's life. I didn't feel that I belonged. When Margot asked me if I needed a table and menu, I said I was just going to sit at the bar and have a drink.

I finished my glass of house red wine, paid, left a tip on the counter, and walked out to the corner of Green and Powell Streets. Even though it was just down the street, I planned no visit to the Green Street Mortuary. I did wonder if the upholstered chairs and little prayer bench were still there. Instead, I decided to take advantage of my three nights in a beautiful hotel. Just then, a taxi let off passengers at Capp's. As they exited the cab, I slid into the back seat and asked the driver to take me to the Mark Hopkins. As before, the doorman greeted the taxi. He opened the back door for me and said, "Welcome back, Mr. Hanlon. I trust you enjoyed your afternoon." I nodded.

Once I returned to my hotel room, I stood at the window to admire the view of the city that *San Francisco Chronicle* journalist Herb Caen called "Bagdad by the Bay." It was a long way down from my hotel room to the street. Some might say it was an even longer way down from San Francisco to Gnome. While I reflected on the sights, I realized that, although I had spent most of my life in San Francisco, it now felt foreign to me. I also understood what the author Thomas Wolfe meant when he wrote *You Can't Go Home Again.*

My hunger had not subsided. If I couldn't go home again, I could order room service, so that's what I did. After I finished my meal, I felt better, especially about my new life in Gnome. There I had new sidewalk spots, and they were my new friends. Now I wondered why I planned to spend more than three days in a city where I no longer had any affinity. Of course, I would attend the reunion. But instead of more time in San Francisco, I decided I would take the train across the bay and explore the sidewalk spots in Berkeley and Oakland. If I had time left over, I might take a ferry across the bay to Sausalito. For years, I had heard about these cities but never visited. Until today, they had no appeal.

I slept better than I had in weeks. The next morning, I didn't wake up until after eleven o'clock. The bed was so comfortable that I decided to stay in it and order room service again. I wasn't sure whether to order breakfast or lunch. I let my stomach decide, and I ordered both. This was the life. If I had enough money, I could be a Nob on full-time basis. It was something to dream about while I waited for room service to knock on the door.

I demolished two eggs, a rasher of bacon, and a cheeseburger, all of which I washed down with a carafe of coffee and glass of coke. I didn't eat the french fries or the toast because I was full. Despite the caffeine from the coffee and coke, I fell back to sleep. When I awoke, it was time to get ready for the reunion.

I planned to wear a navy blue suit. I hoped Mary Ellen would appreciate my gesture. Of course, it was not the same navy blue suit I had worn when I took her to the prom. But it was one I hoped would remind her of our special evening forty years ago. I also planned to wear a white shirt as I had forty years ago and a tie with stripes in colors that, as best I could remember, matched the mauve in her prom dress. I also wanted to buy her a corsage like the one I bought her before, but I changed my mind. I suspected her husband would buy her a corsage, and a second one would be too much, even for Mary Ellen.

Chapter 28
Walkover

Once again, the doorman greeted me as I exited the hotel. "Will you need a taxi, sir?" I nodded. Within minutes, I was on my way to my old high school where I would reunite with classmates after forty years. I wondered if they would look different. Of course, I had seen Nobby just five years before and assumed he would look the same. Although better dressed, he was just as skinny as he had been in high school. I wondered if I would recognize Rusty and Mary Ellen. I wondered what their lives had been like for the last forty years.

When I went through the front doors of the school, the first thing I noticed was the smell. It hadn't changed. It was a unique, somewhat musty smell. It was also an unusual mixture of odors. I detected Pine Sol, a hunt of perspiration from student lockers, radiators, old paint, thick varnish, and too much floor wax. As I made my way down the long corridor and descended the first set of stairs that took me down to the gymnasium entrance, the smell made me feel at home.

As I walked in, I found a table to my right where two young women sat. One asked, "Are you here for the reunion?" I nodded. "Let me sign you in." While I gave her my name and she checked it off a list, the other student completed a name tag for me. Then, in what seemed to be one fluid motion, she stood up, peeled the back off the name tag, and stuck it on the breast pocket of my suit. As she returned to her chair, the first student said the bar was in front of the stage at the other end of the gymnasium. "Have fun!"

As I looked across the gymnasium toward the stage, all I saw was a sea of unrecognizable faces. What if I didn't know anyone? What if my friends had decided not to come? Suddenly, an arm popped out of the crowd and waved. I was relieved to see it was Nobby. As I made my way over to him, I tried to make out names on tags. A few names rang a bell, but they belonged to classmates with whom I had no relationship forty years ago and had no interest in now. Nobby grabbed me and put his arm around my shoulder. "Look at this guy!" he exclaimed. "Who would have ever thought he would amount to anything? Tell Rusty what you've been up to the last forty years."

I hoped my mouth had not dropped, but I'm sure it had when I discovered it was Rusty Swerdlow who stood opposite me. I didn't recognize him. He looked nothing like the tall, handsome, burly football player from high school. As I tried to recover, we shook hands. "It's great to see you, Marcus."

"It's great to see you, too, Rusty. What have you been up to since high school?"

Just then, the woman beside him interjected, "Charles, aren't you going to introduce me to your friend?"

I couldn't remember the last time I had heard Rusty called by his given name. Everyone called him Rusty, even our teachers. Rusty brought his wife in closer. He introduced her to us as Eileen. I discovered they had been married for almost forty years. They met when he was stationed at Fort Ord. Rusty hadn't wasted any time after his high school graduation. He married and quickly had four children. He had also made a career out of the army and retired as Sergeant First Class. For someone who appeared to have a good career in the army, he didn't stand as straight as I would have expected a sergeant to stand. His shoulders were turned forward, his hair was long, and he had a scruffy beard. He looked like someone who didn't care about his appearance. I put it down to his retirement. Just as I gave up suits and neckties, I assumed that when Rusty retired, he gave up his uniform and all that went with it.

As Rusty, Eileen, and I talked, Nobby left and returned with drinks. He had one for each of us. I sipped mine and discovered it was fruit punch. He's one guy I thought would have taken the army and his country by storm. I must have made a face. Nobby came over and whispered in my ear, "No alcohol for our friend Rusty. We have to keep him sober tonight."

Now I knew why Rusty looked so disheveled—he was an alcoholic. He's one guy I thought would have taken the army and then the country by storm. Instead, he looked like a storm had overtaken him.

It became my turn to talk about my past, present, and future. Of course, no one had any interest in insurance. Perhaps it was because they thought I'd want to sell them a policy. Anyway, I glossed over my thirty-five year insurance career. Unlike the army, I explained it was easy to rise through the ranks in an insurance company. In view of Rusty's problem, I was reluctant to say I now owned a liquor store, but I couldn't keep it a secret. Rusty said, "I'm impressed, Marcus. You did well, but I always knew you would." Then he said, "You always kept your head down." I knew what he meant, but in the context of the comments made at my recent anniversary dinner, his comment struck me as a funny.

I asked Rusty about his father and grandmother. Although I meant to be nice, my question was a mistake. By the look on his face, I could tell it brought back painful memories. Rusty told me he left them behind when he left for Fort Ord. He had no idea what had become of either of them. I told Rusty how sorry I was that it had worked out for him that way and told him so. He said, "You were always the lucky one, Marcus. You had a mother who loved you. She showed up for you. My father never showed up except to tell me I was worth nothing or to hit me. And my grandmother was too afraid of my father to intervene." It was tough to know how to respond. What he said was true.

I tried to recover and said, "Well, Rusty, you are blessed with a lovely wife and four children."

Rusty stared straight ahead. "Tell me about your new home and business in Gnome. Would Eileen and I like to live there?" I told them that Gnome was a small town but it liked to think of itself as a city. I couldn't tell if either he or Eileen were interested. Neither reacted. To fill the silence, I offered more details to the extent that I felt I was both an ambassador and a travel agent for Gnome. I even told them how I learned to say Gnome's name. While I thought it was funny, they didn't react. Finally, I gave up and excused myself. I went in search of a real drink, one with alcohol, lots and lots of alcohol. I also went in search of Mary Ellen.

I usually drank red wine, particularly Cabernet Sauvignon. Tonight, though, I ordered a double scotch on the rocks. I didn't even take the time to look at the brand. It didn't matter. I just wanted spirits, any kind, to lift mine after my torturous visit with Rusty and his wife Eileen. I was sorry Nobby had left me alone with them. As I turned away from the bar and took the first welcome sip of my drink, I heard a woman's voice say, "Howdy, stranger. Remember me?" I didn't recognize the face, but I recognized the voice. It was Mary Ellen. She hugged me, and I hugged her back.

Forty years had not been kind to Rusty, but they had been generous to Mary Ellen. I didn't think it was possible. She looked so different but so much better. Her long hair and glasses were gone. While her hair was now short and gray, it was stylish and framed her face. I guessed she now wore contact lenses. For the first time, I saw the magnificence of her blue eyes. She wasn't wearing mauve. Instead, she wore a straight red dress with long sleeves. It accentuated her figure, which had also improved over the years. Why did she ever go to the prom with me? And why did I presume I could buy her corsage, much less have her accept it? Mary Ellen was now what I heard other women call "chic."

"Marcus, I want to introduce you to my husband, Mark Donaldson."
I shook hands with him. He was the type of man I expected Mary
Ellen to marry—tall, slender, and handsome. Mark, like Mary Ellen,
had a full head of gray hair, not one of which was out of place. "I was
so happy to hear you were coming to the reunion, Marcus. At first, I
wasn't sure if Mark and I would attend. But, after Nobby called and
told me you had sent in your check, we signed up right sway."

I was humbled. "Where do you and Mark live, and what do the two
of you do?" The floodgates opened. Mary Ellen took the next twenty
minutes to tell me all about their careers, their travels, and their
family.

After Mary Ellen received her undergraduate degree from Santa
Clara, she had won a scholarship to complete her graduate degree in
psychology at Georgetown University. She met Mark in Georgetown.
He had already graduated with a degree in architecture and worked
for a firm in Washington, D.C. Once Mary Ellen received her
doctorate in psychology, she interned at a hospital before she opened
a private family practice in Georgetown. Mary Ellen said they had
two grown children, a boy named Paul and a girl named Sarah. Both
were married. I was shocked when Mary Ellen said she and Mark
were grandparents. How could so much have happened? Why had I
lost touch with her? She had meant so much to me. Why hadn't I kept
up with her? Just as she did in high school, Mary Ellen radiated self-
assuredness.

A bell rang; it was time for dinner. Mary Ellen put her right arm
through Mark's and her other arm through mine as we walked to the
cafeteria for dinner.

Mary Ellen almost danced with glee when she saw the decorations.
"They have made it so lovely for us, Marcus. Isn't it wonderful?" I had
to agree. For the first time, the cafeteria looked like a place where I
wanted to eat. "What did you order? Steak? Chicken? Fish? Mark and

I ordered fish. We hope it's Petrale sole. It's impossible to find it on the East Coast. Remember, Marcus, we ordered it at Tadich's on prom night? Oh, Mark, we must simply go to Tadich's while we are here." I remembered what I ordered prom night. I just couldn't remember what I had ordered for tonight and told her so. "Why look, Marcus, it's on your name tag. You ordered steak." Just as she had during high school, Mary Ellen kept me on track.

Mary Ellen was effervescent throughout dinner. Both she and Mark engaged me in conversation. They wanted to know what I had done over the past forty years. Did I travel? Was I married? Did I have children? They told me about their travels. I thought they hadn't missed a country. I explained that I traveled for business from time to time when I worked for the insurance company, but now I spend all my time at my business in Gnome. Unlike Rusty and Eileen, Mary Ellen and Mark appeared to be interested in everything I had to say about Gnome, my business, and my home. I told them I had never married and had no children. Mary Ellen stuck out her bottom lip out. "You would have made a great husband and father, Marcus. I hope you aren't too lonely."

Of course, I had my sidewalk spots, but I didn't tell her about them then, just as I hadn't told her about them in high school. Instead, I said, "No, Mary Ellen, I have plenty to keep me busy in Gnome."

Mary Ellen smiled. "I'm happy for you, Marcus."

Nobby was right; the committee had retained an excellent caterer. Mary Ellen raved about the Petrale sole, and I enjoyed my steak. Her husband and our other classmates were just as enthusiastic about their meals and the dessert that followed—strawberry shortcake with whipped cream. After we finished our coffee, the reunion committee chairperson, whom I didn't remember, thanked everyone for their support and made a few comments about what the committee planned to do with any surplus funds from this event. The monies would go toward the cost of new bleachers on the football field. After the chairperson's comments, we went back to the gymnasium for the dance.

I headed for the bar and ordered another double scotch on the rocks. I needed more spirits to boost my own. Why, I wondered? I should be happy. I had renewed friendships with at least two important people from a part of my life when I was happy. I realized my conversation with Rusty was partly to blame. I always thought Rusty was a star. I came to the reunion and expected him to still be a star. He wasn't, and I was disappointed. I knew I wouldn't be a part of his life as it was now. Ironically, my conversation with Mary Ellen was also partly to blame. I always thought Mary Ellen was a star, too. I came to the reunion and expected her to still be star. She was. I was disappointed because I knew there could be no place for me in her life. Two important friends from my past caused a conundrum. They put me in the dumps. I was so out of sorts that I didn't bother to finish my scotch or say goodbye. I simply left the gymnasium and the high school. I walked back to the hotel. If I were lucky, I would be able to see my sidewalk spots under the streetlights. I could talk to them.

I arrived back at the hotel just after nine o'clock. As he held the front door open, the doorman greeted me with "Did you have a pleasant evening, sir?" I nodded. I walked over to the reception desk and informed them I would check out tomorrow morning rather than Monday. I had no need to explore any more of San Francisco or the cities around it. I wanted to go home and take stock of my life.

Chapter 29
Broadside

The drive from San Francisco to Gnome was uneventful. I had slept fitfully, so I was tired. My mood had not improved. I wished I felt better about San Francisco and about the reunion. I wished I felt better about Rusty and Mary Ellen. I wished I felt better about Gnome. Everything left me unsettled about my future. Even my sidewalk spots had let me down on the walk home. They gave me no comfort. I felt that my life needed a shakeup. I planned to think about it more during the next couple of days at home. It had been a while since I had spent any time in my home other than to sleep.

By the time Wednesday morning rolled around, I felt better. I had developed a plan and put it in place. I showered, shaved, dressed, and headed off to work. It was only eight o'clock. I parked in my usual spot. As I got out of my car, I saw the new spots. They looked like cherry or barbeque sauce. As I approached my store, I saw broken glass on the sidewalk in front of my store. I discovered what looked like a robbery.

I called 911 and made a report to the dispatcher. Within a few minutes, the chief of police pulled up. In a city the size of Gnome, it wasn't unusual for the chief to investigate if the other two duty officers were busy. Today, I guessed, was one of those days. If the other officers were busy, I hoped it wasn't a sign of a crime spree in Gnome.

"What happened?" the chief asked. I showed him the broken front window. "Have you been inside?" I said I had just arrived and had seen the blood drops and the broken glass. "Don't go in. We have to preserve the crime scene. I have called for the county's forensic team to come out. They should be here any minute. I have also called for backup." I was surprised by the chief's response. I thought he was melodramatic for what seemed to be a simple robbery.

As he spoke to me, the chief walked to his squad car, opened the trunk, and took out two rolls. One was a large roll of yellow plastic tape with black letters. The other appeared to be gray duct tape. He tied one end of the yellow tape to the drain pipe at the far corner of my store and unrolled it from the pipe around the parking meters and back to the opposite corner, where he affixed it to the wall with a piece of duct tape. The black uppercase letters on the yellow tape said, "CRIME SCENE DO NOT CROSS." The chief then returned the gray and yellow rolls to the trunk of his car. Before closing the lid, he took out a stack of florescent red plastic cones. "Show me where the blood drops are." As I pointed each one out, the chief placed a red cone on top. "The crime scene is preserved for now."

Just after the chief had placed the last cone, the county forensic team arrived. I'm not sure why, but I was surprised by how meticulous they were. This was Gnome, not San Francisco. One technician photographed the entire scene as well as the blood drops. A second technician picked up and bagged the glass in front of the store, while a third technician took scrapes from each of the blood spots and placed them in individual plastic tubes. Yet a fourth technician dusted and captured fingerprints from around the window and on the front door. All technicians recorded their activities in a log and catalogued any bags, bottles, tubes, or papers. After they were finished outside, I gave the chief my key so they could go inside the store.

The police chief and forensic technicians were in the store for several hours. All I could do was wait, although I was kept busy. The red lights flashed on both the chief's car and the county's forensic van. They attracted a crowd. Onlookers had questions, and I did my best to try to answer them. Margie showed up for work and was shocked by what she saw. Together, we stood and commiserated. After a while, one of my customers brought us cups of coffee, for which we were grateful. As we sipped our coffees, people wondered out loud who had been so bold as to rob my store. "This city has really changed, and not for the better," lamented Margie.

While the forensic team packed up, the police chief asked me to sit in his car. He had questions for me, and he made room for me on the front seat. "Our first order of business is to eliminate suspects. We will need fingerprints and blood samples from you and your employees."

I was shocked that the chief would consider any of us as suspects. "Why would anyone want to rob their own place of business?" I asked. "Why would employees want to take advantage of their employer?"

"You have no idea what I see in this line of business. People do all kinds of strange things. While the forensic team is still here, they will fingerprint and take blood samples from you. And, isn't that Margie over there? We'll take her fingerprints and blood sample, too. If you could get the other employees to come to the store now, it would save us time. Here, you can use my portable phone."

I was able to reach Sandra right away, and she came downtown in a matter of minutes. I left Tony a message on his answering machine. By the time the technicians were through with me, Margie, and Sandra, Tony showed up. "I was sound asleep when you called. What's going on?"

By three o'clock, the forensic technicians had taken our fingerprints and blood samples. We were scheduled to give statements to the police later in the day. Meanwhile, we had to cover the broken window and sweep up the rest of the mess. Tony measured the window and headed to the hardware store for a sheet of plywood. Together, we mounted it on the outside wall. It wasn't attractive, but it would do until a glazer could come. Margie and Sandra washed away some of the fingerprint dust, but they knew they had more work to do. After we had done all we could for the day, I left for the police station. I wanted to get my statement behind me.

The chief invited me into an interview room. For some reason, I thought we would sit in his office as we had done in the past when we met to discuss Chamber of Commerce and Kiwanis club events. I now realized the seriousness of his investigation. He began with questions about my activities over the last few days. I told him about my reunion. He wanted to know with whom I had spent time. "Do I need an alibi?" I asked.

The chief explained that crimes were often committed by someone we know. "To us, it looks like an inside job." Based on the evidence, the chief and forensic technicians had reason to believe the robbery may have been committed by someone with inside knowledge about the store and its contents. He wanted names of people with whom I had spoken at the reunion.

I started to panic. What would my classmates think of me if the police contacted them? I thought about Rusty and Nobby. I knew Rusty was an alcoholic. Both he and his wife had wanted to know about my business and Gnome. Could the police chief think Rusty and Eileen were involved? Nobby's career had brought him into contact with sketchy characters and probably law enforcement. And he always had lots of questions about my business. Could the police chief think Nobby was involved? Mary Ellen and Mark Donaldson were professionals and pillars of their community. Could the police chief think they were involved? Never! The idea that the police would contact any of my former classmates mortified me. However, I could tell the chief didn't care what I thought. He wanted answers to his questions. I made a list of everyone with whom I had been in contact.

The next day, the store window was replaced, and the four of us cleaned up. My insurance agent stopped by, and he helped me complete claim forms. Although I had spent thirty-five years in insurance, my experience had been limited to life and health. I knew nothing about property insurance. So I relied on Phil to guide me when I bought the store from him. I kept his insurance agent and policy. Each year, my agent told me how much coverage I needed and how much I needed to pay.

The other businesses around me washed down their sidewalks so the blood spots disappeared. I was grateful my sidewalk spots remained unspoiled. Within a few days, interest in the robbery waned. After a couple of weeks, we went about our business as if nothing had happened. Just the same, Margie and Sandra were worried. They wanted me to install an alarm system. I told them I would think about it. Customers still expressed concern, but as time went on, we became more relaxed. My sidewalk spots helped me get through it. They were all I needed.

From time to time, I would run into our police chief and ask him about developments. He usually just shrugged his shoulders and said, "Nothing yet. These things take time, but we have a pretty good track record."

The next time I saw the chief was the day he pulled up in his police car in front of my store. He sat for a few minutes before he opened his door. He exited his car and hiked up his pants. He saw me as I stood and looked out the front window. He offered what looked like a two-finger salute. I waved back. Then, he lifted his right index and middle finger and pulled them toward him, signaling for me to come outside. I wondered if today was the day he would give me an update.

I walked out my front door to the sidewalk. I noticed the chief stood on one of my favorite sidewalk spots, but I didn't try to get him to move. As we stood face to face, the chief told me the forensic team had completed its tests. "We analyzed the fingerprints and blood samples. We assessed everyone's statements and the rest of the information in our case file. I am proud of the work our investigative team has done to solve this case." Did he just say solve? I didn't know what to think. I was surprised and shocked.

"Mr. Hanlon, as you recall, the broken window glass was scattered all over the sidewalk when I arrived on the scene. The forensic team found no glass fragments inside the store. This told us the glass was smashed from the inside, not the outside. The front door was intact and locked, which meant someone had used a key to enter and exit. During their forensic examination of the glass fragments, the technicians discovered blood on some pieces. This blood matched the stains on the trail from your store to the parking lot. We compared the results of those blood samples with those we took from you and your staff. The results of all these tests, comparisons, and evidence confirm our initial suspicion. The robbery was an inside job." I was thunderstruck. I didn't know what to say.

"Mr. Hanlon, I am here to arrest you for burglary, false statements, misleading a police investigation, and insurance fraud." I shook my head, I couldn't believe it. I thought my plan had been foolproof. All I wanted was some attention. All I wanted was to shake things up. Not this. The chief put his hand to his belt and reached for his handcuffs.

I ran. I don't remember the sound of the tires as they tried to screech to a halt. I don't remember the thump of the F150 Ford pickup truck as it hit my rib cage. I don't remember the sensation as I somersaulted to the curb. I don't remember how I flew out of my brown Rockport soft-soled shoes. I don't remember my screams of anguish as my body hit the concrete face first.

But I do remember my joy when I opened my eyes and saw my beloved sidewalk spots. We were together at last.

Acknowledgments

Sidewalk Spots is a work of fiction. All characters are fictitious except Joe Capp. Mr. Capp was a real person. At one time, he owned Capp's Corners. I visited Capp's Corners countless times between1992 and 2015. Capp's closed in April 2015. Although I never met Joe Capp, I have tried to capture him in the ways he has been described to me by others including his late daughter, Cheryl Capp. I became acquainted with Cheryl Capp when she worked in Lincoln, CA. I hope my depiction of Joe Capp enhances the esteem in which he is held.

My heartfelt appreciation is extended to Flore Baudouin, Valerie Bedford, Jeri Chase Ferris and Helen Christensen who read an early draft of Sidewalk Spots. Their insights, comments and suggestions helped make Sidewalk Spots a better book.

A special thanks goes to Paul Shelgren, (Ret.) Chief of Police at City of Lincoln, CA.

I am grateful to Kathy Looper who took me on a walking tour of San Francisco's Tenderloin and shared its history. Ms. Looper is Executive Director of Reality House West which owns the historic Cadillac Hotel, the first "Single Residence Occupancy"(SRO) hotel west of the Mississippi. The Cadillac Hotel is located in the heart of the Tenderloin. Kathy Looper is an active community volunteer. She and her late husband Leroy Looper have dedicated her lives to helping people down on their luck. Ms. Looper also serves as Board President of The Tenderloin Museum, 398 Eddy Street, San Francisco. For more information about the museum, visit tenderloinmuseum.org.

I also wish to thank those who read the final draft of Sidewalk Spots. Their names and comments appear on the back cover.

It can be difficult to get a book published. Once again, I counted on the support and expertise of Freiling Literary Agency to bring Sidewalk Spots to print. Thank you Tom Freiling, Deborah Thomas and Mark Lalumondier.